AFGHAN
The Script

AFGHAN
The Script

by

Nigel Clayton

Published in Australia by Zuytdorp Press, 2021

Afghan
ISBN 978-0-6454632-9-3

DRA012000 DRAMA / Australian & Oceanian
FIC014000 FICTION / Historical / General
FIC002000 FICTION / Action & Adventure

Epic poems by this author:

Afghan - Song of the Desert
Orcinus Orca - Song of the Ocean
Hollandia Nova - Song of the Coast
Kibeho - An Epic Poem
Song of the Templar [poetic verse]
Songs of Australia - A Poetic Trilogy
1453 - Constantinople

Other titles by this author:

The Long Road to Rwanda
The Templar: and the City of God [Part 1]
The Templar: and the Temple of Káros [Part 2]
The Templar: and the Cross of Christ [Part 3]
Amazon [Part 4 of The Templar series]
Chivalry [Omnibus]
Underworld
Templar, Assassination, Trial & Torture
Dreamtime - An Aboriginal Odyssey
The Zuytdorp Survivors
Afghan Camel Strings and the Australian Outback
Tom of Twofold Bay
This Pestilence, Bergen-Belsen
Afghan: The Script
Colonies of Earth: also known as Mildratawa
Fall of the Inca Empire
Kibeho: Original Script
The Kibeho Massacre: As It Happened
Furious George

EXT.CHAR ASIAB - DAY

SUPERIMPOSED: CHAR ASIAB, 6 OCTOBER, 1879

Three British field guns fire from a ridge. British
Highlanders, Gurkhas, and the 5th Punjab Infantry approach
the Afghan defensive position.

SUPREIMPOSED FADES

The British lines are steady and advance slowly at first.
The desert explodes in places as the fire from the field guns
takes effect, but does little damage to the Afghan defenses.

The British forces continue to close the gap and the Afghans
return fire, putting up a stiff resistance.

Afghan and British dead commence to litter the desert,
screams from the dying fill the air, and the British continue
the advance. Volley after volley of rifle fire rains havoc
and the battle noise is deafening.

A final explosion from a field gun fills the air and we are
consumed by a smoke-filled screen.

FADE TO BLACK.

EXT. TRAIN STATION - DAY

SUPERIMPOSED: MARREE, AUSTRALIA, JANUARY 1884

We rush across the barren desert and slowly descend upon the
main street, where a police station with its three officers
come into view. We continue on past other buildings of
Marree.

SUPERIMPOSED FADES

A camel string with their Afghan handlers is seen as it
passes a bullock team, the Afghans receiving a cold stare
from the Australian handlers.

We follow a bend in the road and come across the train
station, the end of the line. Several Australian men can be
seen on the platform, heavily tanned by the conditions of the
desert, flies becoming visible, pestering their victims.

Two Aboriginals are seated upon the scorched earth beneath a
tree on the far side of the railway track. A lone Afghan
stands upon the platform.

The Afghan is NAK KADIR, 42, sunburnt and thin. His gums are
well parted from his teeth, teeth stained brown.

His lips are scarred, a permanent grimace forced upon him.

The scar extends up the right side of his face. He's waiting
for the arrival of ABDUL HASSAN, 27 years of age.

Nak looks down the line. The train finally comes into view.
He brushes away several flies from his face.

INT. TRAIN - DAY

Abdul rocks with the motion of the train, the brakes heard
over the whistling of steam. His hands rest freely upon his
lap. He is alone in the cabin.

Abdul's face fills the screen. He is very handsome and fresh,
well-tanned and clean. He sits erect and is smiling. His
smile then fades.

Abdul peers out of the train window and he sees Nak. Abdul's
Adam's apple moves as he swallows a little nervousness away.

EXT. TRAIN STATION - MOMENTS LATER

The train's braking now fills the air. The Australian men,
faces of steel, stop in mid conversation.

The train slows and stops, doors along its length open, and
seven people disembark. Nak notices a lone figure getting out
of one of the carriages, he's wearing a turban. Nak awaits
Abdul's approach.

They speak in their native tongue.

                    NAK (SUBTITLE)
          Are you Abdul Hassan?

                    ABDUL (SUBTITLE)
          Yes... I'm Abdul.

Abdul is staring at Nak. Nak subconsciously rubs at the scar
on his mouth and cheek with his left hand.

                    NAK (SUBTITLE)
          I'm Nak Kadir.

They shake hands.

                    ABDUL (SUBTITLE)
          I'm happy to meet you.

                    NAK (SUBTITLE)
          Do you have much baggage?

                    ABDUL (SUBTITLE)
          No, nothing at all.

                    NAK (SUBTITLE)
          What; nothing?

An Australian walks past and gives a cold and hard stare. Nak
ignores it. Abdul slowly looks away.

                    ABDUL (SUBTITLE)
          My only baggage was stolen several
          days ago; all I have are the
          clothes on my back. I came as soon
          as I could. I'm a hard worker.

                    NAK (SUBTITLE)
          Please... come with me, Abdul. I'll
          take you to meet Shir Adji. He'll
          be pleased to see you've arrived
          safely.
                    (beat)
          I'm sorry to hear about your
          belongings.

                    ABDUL (SUBTITLE)
                    (trying to be optimistic)
          It wasn't much.

They commenced walking along the platform and through to the
main street of Marree.

EXT. MAIN STREET - CONTINUOUS

Abdul continues to feel uneasy and breaks the silence as he
waves his hand across his face, walking side by side, he and
Nak.

                    ABDUL (SUBTITLE)
          I see the flies are as bad here as
          they are anywhere else in this
          country.

                    NAK (SUBTITLE)
          You'll get used to them.

Anxiety is present. Abdul rubs his left forearm up and down.

                    ABDUL (SUBTITLE)
          I've heard that work is good here.

                    NAK (SUBTITLE)
          It's good, so long as you don't
          mind working for little more than
          nothing.

                    ABDUL (SUBTITLE)
               (hopeful)
          But better than being in
          Afghanistan I hope.
               (beat)
          I've a wife in Afghanistan, and two
          children.

Nak looks Abdul in the eye and can see his pain. He can see
his insecurity.

                    NAK (SUBTITLE)
          Don't worry, Abdul. You'll survive.
          Just stay away from men like Faiz
          Mahomet, or you'll soon be drowned
          in your own sorrows. There's money
          to be made, but it won't come
          easily, but despite my poor view in
          regards to money... yes, it's there
          be made.

A bullock team passes them, a cloud of dust rising quickly to
engulf them as they walk.

Two white Australians in the background look towards Nak and
Abdul, and one of them spits in their direction before
resuming his conversation with his friend.

                    ABDUL (SUBTITLE)
               (nervously)
          When's our first job?

                    NAK (SUBTITLE)
          We'll depart tomorrow morning for a
          homestead near Birdsville. We have
          a few smaller stops along the way,
          but nothing too awkward or timeconsuming.
               (beat)
          So, Abdul... you're from Kandahar I
          hear?

                    ABDUL (SUBTITLE)
          Yes... yes I am, but only recently;
          two years.

Two elderly women stand nearby. Elderly WOMAN #1, 50 years of
age, turns her head to WOMAN #2, her friend who is 49.

                    WOMAN #1
          They're so dirty.

                    WOMAN #2
          Oh, I agree. An absolutely
          disgusting lot if you ask me.

The comment means nothing to Nak, words so easily ignored,
and Abdul pretends not to hear the women, but his eyes,
moving from left to right, betray him.

                    NAK (SUBTITLE)
          I'm from Kabul and Shir is from
          Karachi.

                    ABDUL (SUBTITLE)
          Did you leave Afghanistan before
          the British moved into that region,
          or after?

                    NAK (SUBTITLE)
          After.

Nak looks around before continuing.

                    NAK (SUBTITLE) (CONT'D)
          I fought in action against the
          British and came to this country
          just over three years ago.

                    ABDUL (SUBTITLE)
               (jokingly)
          And now you serve them.

                    NAK (SUBTITLE)
               (angrily at first)
          I serve no one.... We might be
          looked upon as though we're little
          more than peasants in this country,
          but we're not peasants, Abdul...
          remember that; always.

                    ABDUL (SUBTITLE)
          I'm sorry; I... I took up a
          tribesman's life back home... after
          many years of adventure.

                    NAK (SUBTITLE)
          I know that much, and that's about
          it... my friend in Adelaide told me
          a little.

                    ABDUL (SUBTITLE)
          And about your position here, Nak?
               (beat)
          Aren't you concerned about being
          discovered as an enemy of the
          British.

Nak pauses for a moment as he looks around once more and
stares into Abdul's eyes as they continue on their way.

                    NAK (SUBTITLE)
No. I've escaped them now.

                    ABDUL (SUBTITLE)
Australia's but part of the British
Empire. There's no escaping it.

                    NAK (SUBTITLE)
No escaping it.... Maybe you're
right. But I'm happy. I've found my
place in life.

A feeling of discomfort befalls them both

                    ABDUL (SUBTITLE)
                  (after a pause)
I served with General Robert's
Camel Transport Corps. I was in the
march of 1880, from Kabul to
Kandahar.

Abdul is staring again at Nak.

                    ABDUL (SUBTITLE) (CONT'D)
You served against the British and
I served with them.

Nak stops dead in his tracks, followed quickly by Abdul. Nak
then resumes the walk once more, Abdul alongside.

                    NAK (SUBTITLE)
Tell me, why did you decide to
accept my job offer?

                    ABDUL (SUBTITLE)
It seemed to be the right
decision.... There's so many men
and camels bottle-necked in
Adelaide with nowhere to go. A man
grabbed me on the arm and... well;
he persuaded me quite easily.
Besides, I needed work... everyone
needs work.

                    NAK (SUBTITLE)
Jehangir. He's a good man. He's
half Indian; could you tell?

                    ABDUL (SUBTITLE)
No, not really.
     (beat)
My own father was from India, but
my mother's an Afghani, brought up
                  (MORE)

                (CONT'D)
     in a small village between Peshawar
     and Jalalabad. My father used to
     say. 'a rose between two thorns'.

Abdul is hesitating.

                ABDUL (SUBTITLE) (CONT'D)
     I felt it my duty to honor him,
     that's why I served in the Punjab
     Infantry, and before you can ask,
     the answer is yes, I do feel a
     little dirty for all I've done in
     my past, but that is behind me now,
     and I'm looking for a new future.
          (beat)
     I swear this upon my parent's
     grave.

                NAK (SUBTITLE)
     We served those we needed to serve
     in order to find our place in life,
     but now... now we serve ourselves.
     Forget it... forget it all...
     please. War is a strange bedfellow.

                ABDUL (SUBTITLE)
     What about Shir?

                NAK (SUBTITLE)
     We don't speak of the war any more.

Abdul pauses for a moment as the walk continues.

                ABDUL (SUBTITLE)
     I'm sorry, Nak. I just feel as
     though I need to explain myself,
     given the situation... you and I.
     I'm not proud for anything I've
     done, but proud to have served a
     sworn duty to my father, but I no
     longer embrace the past.

                NAK (SUBTITLE)
     Forget it, Abdul; all of it;
     please. We're at peace now, both of
     us.

                ABDUL (SUBTITLE)
     Thank you, Nak. I appreciate
     this... this honor which you've
     provided me.

                    NAK (SUBTITLE)
          Think nothing of it.
                (beat)
          Did I tell you, Shir's to be
          married; tonight?

                    ABDUL (SUBTITLE)
          Is she a woman from our home
          country?

                    NAK (SUBTITLE)
          No, she's from here. She's an
          Aboriginal.

                    ABDUL (SUBTITLE)
          Shir must be happy to be getting
          married. So hard it is to find love
          in this world of ours.

There is a short pause before Nak responds, he seems to be
hiding something.

                    NAK (SUBTITLE)
          I couldn't agree more.

Nak's cheeks then lift slightly, as though he's smiling to
himself, but it's too hard to tell due to his facial injury.

                    NAK (SUBTITLE) (CONT'D)
          You're invited to the wedding, of
          course. Shir wouldn't dream of
          forcing you to an evening alone...
          most of the Afghan community will
          be there.

INT. WAREHOUSE - CONTINUOUS

SHIR ADJI, 33 years of age, has a deformed nose filled with
potholes, high cheekbones and shallow cheeks, rather ugly and
seemingly filled with an hatred for all of mankind.

He's checking supplies upon his list; bags, sacks and tins;
sugar, rice, vegetables, oatmeal, potatoes, tea, baking
powder, and much more. Shir turns to see Nak and Abdul enter
the warehouse.

                    SHIR (SUBTITLE)
          Ah, this must be Abdul.

They close the gap and shake hands.

                    ABDUL (SUBTITLE)
          I'm very pleased to be here.

                    SHIR (SUBTITLE)
The pleasure is ours... times are
hard, but you'll find it all very
rewarding. There's much experience
to be had here in the Australian
desert.

                    ABDUL (SUBTITLE)
I'm an eager man, Shir, and I've
had a lot of experience with camels
back home, and crossed my fair
share of deserts.

Two Australians walk past in the background, a look of
disgust falling over them, their faces displaying much
displeasure towards the Afghans. Abdul is uncomfortable.

                    SHIR (SUBTITLE)
Desert here, desert there... but
you're right, it's much the same
wherever you go, only the camels
change... as do the handlers.

                    NAK (SUBTITLE)
Shir is referring to the colonists.
They're stupid, one and all. There
isn't a single man amongst the
Europeans that can do nearly as
good a job as any of us when it
comes to handling a string of
camels.

Nak looks around to see the stores piled high.

                    NAK (SUBTITLE) (CONT'D)
You've nearly finished, Shir.

                    SHIR (SUBTITLE)
I've a wedding to attend to, or did
you forget?

                    NAK (SUBTITLE)
How could I forget?
     (to Abdul)
He's been reminding me every day
for the past week.

                    SHIR (SUBTITLE)
Come on... help me finish with this
lot; just a few minutes work
remains and we can be off to
prepare for tonight's feast. You're
invited, too, Abdul.

                    ABDUL (SUBTITLE)
          Thank you, Shir; Nak mentioned it.

                    SHIR (SUBTITLE)
          Come on, I've almost finished.
               (beat)
          Oh, Nak, did you explain to Abdul
          about our prayers whilst
          delivering?

                    NAK (SUBTITLE)
          No; thanks for reminding me.
               (beat)
          You finish up, Shir.

Shir briefly holds up his right hand and commences to finish
with his work as Nak explains things to Abdul.

                    NAK (SUBTITLE) (CONT'D)
          Abdul, when doing deliveries,
          especially during summer, we don't
          stop for prayer. We pray twice a
          day, only two of the pillars given
          respect: Salut-ul-Fajr and Salutul-
          Maghrib.

                    ABDUL (SUBTITLE)
          That's okay, Nak... It makes sense,
          really.

                    NAK (SUBTITLE)
          I wish it could be more but the
          camels don't like to stand in the
          middle of the day with heat bearing
          down upon them, and with a heavy
          loud on their backs... and we don't
          use water for ablution; prior to
          prayer we pile a small mound of
          sand beside us and use this to
          symbolize our washing.

                    ABDUL (SUBTITLE)
          I heard people talking in Adelaide
          and suspected as much. I think I
          also heard mention of them facing
          the north-west

                    NAK (SUBTITLE)
          As most appear to do, but it's a
          delicate subject. Mecca is closer
          to Australia from that direction.
          The jemadar of each string usually
          makes up the rules regards prayer,
                    (MORE)

                    (CONT'D)
          and being jemadar myself I don't
          take such rules lightly.
                    (beat)
          I'll look after you, Abdul; both me
          and Shir will help you along the
          way. You're in good hands, trust
          me.

                    ABDUL (SUBTITLE)
                    (smiling)
          I couldn't be happy to hear you say
          that, Nak. Prayers during the
          morning and at sunset are also
          those I look forward to the most.

                    NAK (SUBTITLE)
          Well then, that's settled, but if
          you have any questions, Abdul,
          please ask and never keep them to
          yourself. Now; let's see if Shir is
          ready so that we can be on our way;
          or we can stand back and watch.

They look each other in the eye.

                    ABDUL (SUBTITLE)
          Let's help.

                                        DISSOLVE TO:

INT. MOSQUE - NIGHT

The mirab faced Mecca, a koran lay at its front, wrapped and
positioned upon a stool. Lanterns hang from the roof. Shir
and the other 23 men kneel in prayer as they face it. At the
conclusion of their prayers they each stand and move out
through the door of the mosque and into the stillness of the
night.

EXT. MOSQUE - CONTINUOUS

The singing of cicadas fills the air. The men move around to
the front of the main hall and enter, two at a time.

INT. MAIN HALL - MOMENTS LATER

It's now that the friendly chatter grows, men greeted by the
women. a small feast is set upon many tables in the tinroofed
building of meager worth.

Shir considers his wife, ARIKA, 18, plump and beautiful. Her
hair is black and skin very dark. They smile at one another
and move closer.

MONTAGE

The MULLAH of Marree is 52 years old and ready to perform his
duties in the ceremony. He stands before the couple to be
married.
Shir and Arika hold hands.

Vows are exchanged, Arika acts by prompt.

The couples eyes lock and they kiss, and the Mullah makes the
announcement of their union.

The guests applaud.

END MONTAGE

An elderly guest of important status, a man named ZAREEN,
approaches Shir and Arika. He hands over an envelope.

                    ZAREEN (SUBTITLE)
          My best wishes to you and your new
          wife, Shir. May Allah bestow upon
          you many favors. Please accept this
          small gift on behalf of us all.

                    SHIR (SUBTITLE)
          Thank you, Zareen.
               (to the guests)
          Thank you, one and all.

Nak moves in from the side and stands beside the couple.

                    NAK (SUBTITLE)
          It's with the great honor bestowed
          upon me, that I offer to you all,
          this wonderful array of
          refreshments...

Nak indicates the feast upon the tables.

                    NAK (SUBTITLE) (CONT'D)
          As was prepared by you all.

The guests applaud once more.

                    NAK (SUBTITLE) (CONT'D)
          Please help yourselves, and if your
          name wasn't on the guest list, then
          keep your hands in your pockets.

The guests laugh.

                    SHIR (SUBTITLE)
          Yes, thank you one and all for
          attending this day.

Shir looks into his wife's eyes momentarily.

                    SHIR (SUBTITLE) (CONT'D)
          It means so much to us both.

Again the guests applaud, all seemingly happy and cheerful.

                    SHIR (SUBTITLE) (CONT'D)
          Please... eat, eat, all of you.

                                        DISSOLVE TO:

INT. MAIN HALL - LATER

Nak and Abdul stand before Shir and Arika.

                    NAK (SUBTITLE)
          We're going to depart now, Shir. I
          wish you both the very best,
          although your time together will be
          short...

Nak turns to Arika and speaks the best English he can.

                    NAK (CONT'D)
          Tomorrow we go, no come back for a
          long time; is a four week journey.

Arika simply smiles contentedly.

                    SHIR (SUBTITLE)
               (smiling)
          She knows, Nak.

                    NAK (SUBTITLE)
          Of course... sorry.

                    ABDUL (SUBTITLE)
          And I'd like to thank you both...
          and Arika.

Arika smiles again on hearing her name mentioned.

                    ABDUL (SUBTITLE) (CONT'D)
          I've had a wonderful time here. The
          people of the ghantown are simply
          wonderful. I'm looking forward to
          spending many years here.

                    SHIR (SUBTITLE)
          Thank you for coming, Abdul. I'll
          see you and Nak in the morning.
               (beat)
          Oh, I almost forgot. I've several
                    (MORE)

                    (CONT'D)
          letters which I have to give you,
          Nak; letters for the homestead
          when we arrive in Birdsville.

                    NAK (SUBTITLE)
          You shouldn't be thinking of work
          at a time like this. Go and spend
          what little time you have,
          together... go, go on.

                    SHIR (SUBTITLE)
          You're right, of course.
               (smiling at Arika)
          What'll you be doing tonight, Nak?

                    NAK (SUBTITLE)
          Nothing that should be concerning
          you, dear friend.

                    ARIKA
               (poorly spoken English)
          All nearly go home. We go too,
          soon. Is time for us. Wait no
          longer, look to first night with
          husband.

Nak holds Arika's hand momentarily and then releases it.
We close in on Nak's eyes as they sparkle in the light given
off by a lantern.

                                        MATCH CUT TO:

EXT. IRON SHACK - NIGHT

Nak's eye fills the screen and we then see him standing
outside a small shack. Nak sees a single article of clothing
hanging over the clothes line, an undershirt. He smiles to
himself on seeing this flag. He takes it from the line before
stepping towards the wooden door and knocks. He looks over
his shoulders, left and right. Several date trees grow
nearby.

Nak is seeking the company of SAKI, a beautiful and young
Japanese prostitute in her early 20's. She opens the door
slightly and smiles through the crack, shadows folding across
her half hidden face.

She recognizes Nak and opens the door, her slender body
coming to view. They exchange pleasantries in broken English.

                    NAK
          Is good night out, a cool breeze.

                    SAKI
          Yes... it is good. Please, you come
          in.

Nak enters, Saki closes the door behind him.

INT. IRON SHACK - CONTINUOUS

A single lantern illuminates dimly the only room of the iron
shack, a bed catches Nak's eyes, a wool rug beside the bed. A
bench top and water basin also exists. Nak turns to face
Saki.

                    NAK
          I go tomorrow, go long time; come
          back is four weeks.

                    SAKI
          I'm happy to know I see you when
          you come back, Nak.

                    NAK
          I like to stay all night with Saki.

Nak pulls a fold of money from his pocket. Saki pushes his
hand aside.

Saki moves over to the bed, taking Nak by the hand. He
follows.

They stand facing each other. Saki pulls the bow of her silk
gown and the gown falls away, revealing her breasts in the
dim light. Nak looks down and Saki kisses his right cheek
tenderly. Their hands move up and down each others body.

                                        FADE TO BLACK.

EXT. WAREHOUSE - MORNING

The sun is rising above the horizon, shimmering waves of heat
dance across the contours of the land. Muslim prayer from the
ghantown can be heard upon the fresh breeze of the morning.
Nak comes into view as he approaches Abdul and Shir.

                    SHIR (SUBTITLE)
          Good morning to you, Nak.

                    NAK (SUBTITLE)
          Good morning to you both. I hope
          your night was a comfortable one,
          Shir.

Shir smiles at the comment.

                    NAK (SUBTITLE) (CONT'D)
          And how was your night, Abdul? Did
          you have enough time for prayer?

                    ABDUL (SUBTITLE)
          Wonderful; and yes, I've prayed. I
          can't thank you enough for finding
          me a host family. The home of Bauz
          was most obliging and friendly.

                    NAK (SUBTITLE)
          All in Marree are obliging, unless
          they're white and speak fluent
          English.

The three men now stand within arm's reach.

                    NAK (SUBTITLE) (CONT'D)
               (to Shir)
          You look wonderfully refreshed.

                    SHIR (SUBTITLE)
          Refreshed and tired.
               (beat)
          You, too, look somewhat...
          refreshed.

                    NAK (SUBTITLE)
          I sought the good company of an old
          friend last night.

Nak looks over Shir's shoulder.

                    NAK (SUBTITLE) (CONT'D)
          I see that you've got the boy hard
          at work.

Shir and Abdul both turn to see GOULAM, an Aboriginal
teenager of 15 years, bringing the 24 camels before the
stores upon the ground.

                    SHIR (SUBTITLE)
          He needs to learn to work as anyone
          else.

Shir faces Nak and hands him two letters.

                    SHIR (SUBTITLE) (CONT'D)
          I was handed these by the Post
          Master late yesterday.

                    NAK (SUBTITLE)
          Huh; late as usual.
               (to Abdul)
               (MORE)

              (CONT'D)
The news travels fast here in
Marree. The Post Master likes to
know the business of everyone in
town, and in no real hurry to help
an Afghan.

           SHIR (SUBTITLE)
        (to Abdul)
Believe me, if this letter
concerned a settlement owned by
Muslims, then they wouldn't be
late; they'd be missing. The
Europeans... always the same...
they have such little respect for
Afghans.

           NAK (SUBTITLE)
But these letters, Abdul, could be
worth a lot, possibly an order of
more wool than we're expected to
pick up... a bigger wage when the
task is complete.

           SHIR (SUBTITLE)
Yes, there's always that. But let's
talk on this a little later...
we've camels to move and supplies
to attend.

          ABDUL (SUBTITLE)
Great. I'm looking forward to my
first real day of work.

           SHIR (SUBTITLE)
And it won't be your last. If we
can provide good service here then
we'll sure to land another job.
Good news travels slow; bad news
travels exceedingly fast.

SERIES OF SHOTS

The string of camels is taking shape. Camels sniff their
packs wearily.

Stores are being loaded from front to back as the camels sit.
The kitchen camel is to the rear of the line and loaded last.
Camels are connected neck to neck with long rope and wooden
nose pegs.

Nak kisses the camels upon the lips as he moves up and down
the line.

END SERIES OF SHOTS

RETURN TO SCENE

We see Abdul looking down the line of camels.

                    ABDUL (SUBTITLE)
               (to Nak)
          You've got a pregnant camel

                    NAK (SUBTITLE)
          She'll be giving birth in a few
          days.

                    ABDUL (SUBTITLE)
          It's not my place, but wouldn't she
          be best left behind?

                    NAK (SUBTITLE)
          My camels are all good camels, all
          are hard workers.
               (beat)
          The mother will carry the extra
          load without question and after a
          few days of whining the new arrival
          will soon settle down. Besides, we
          can't afford to leave her behind,
          and the string works best when the
          order of march hasn't been tampered
          with. All know their place within
          the string.
               (beat)
          The eight currently in the center
          of the string as you see them are
          your responsibility, Abdul. They're
          your children; look after them and
          they'll look after you.

                    ABDUL (SUBTITLE)
          Do they have names?

                    NAK (SUBTITLE)
          Of course they have names. Who
          would I be not to name them? You'll
          get better acquainted with them all
          during the move north, but the one
          closest to you is Amaroo. The one
          behind is Girra.
               (beat)
          It's the name given to an
          Australian creek or tree, but I
          don't know which.

                    SHIR (SUBTITLE)
          Amaroo means, a beautiful place...
          a strange name for a male, if you
          ask me.

                    NAK (SUBTITLE)
                 (ignoring Shir)
          For the moment you might have to
          rely on your stick.

                    SHIR (SUBTITLE)
          Aye; a good sting to the neck
          always clears the mind and
          reinforces discipline.

                    NAK (SUBTITLE)
          Come on, Abdul. Time to get them
          up.

Commands are given, the camels respond and stand.

        NAK (SUBTITLE) (CONT'D)   SHIR (SUBTITLE)
     Get up, all of you. Up! Up!   Come, little ones, time to
                                      move now.

Abdul looks down the line at the eight under his control. He
looks at Nak and Shir, their camels stand, his do not.

                    ABDUL (SUBTITLE)
          Mine must be lazy, there's still
          six that haven't moved.

                    NAK (SUBTITLE)
          They're testing you... that's all.
          Show them who's boss and they'll
          learn fast enough.

                    ABDUL (SUBTITLE)
          Should I use my stick?

                    NAK (SUBTITLE)
          Do what you want, Abdul; that's
          what it's for; but some free
          advice... be fair, for my camels
          will remember, and they'll find
          some way to get even with you in
          the end.

                    SHIR (SUBTITLE)
          They're almost human. Better
          trained then the Australian men in
          town and better tempered than their
          women.

Nak and Shir continue tending to their camels and laugh a
little as Abdul gets his animals to their feet.

SERIES OF SHOTS

A muzzle is attached to one animal.

Nose pegs are double-checked.

Pouches and bags are pulled to ensure they aren't loose.

Goulam stands with his hands on his hips.

END SERIES OF SHOTS

RETURN TO SCENE

Nak reaches into his pocket and reveals a coin for Goulam, who runs to receive his reward with a smile, and employs reasonably good English.

                    GOULAM
          Thank you, thank you much... thank
          you, Nak. You generous, not like
          the white fellah.

Goulam runs off, jumps into the air, and disappears from view.

Nak turns to the others.

                    NAK (SUBTITLE)
          It's time to get going whilst the
          morning's still young. Let's get
          this string on the desert path to
          nowhere.

Shir moves down the line to take position with the rear most camels, and Abdul squares off in the center, where his eye falls upon Nak as he pulls a rifle from within a rolled blanket.

Nak looks it over briefly, fondles with the trigger and sights, and then rolls it back up and secures it into place under several straps.

Abdul looks at Shir who catches his stare.

                    SHIR (SUBTITLE)
          Don't worry, Abdul. We've plenty of
          jerked meat, but if needed, Nak
          will see to it that we're fed well.
          He's a good shot.
                    (raising his voice)
          Aren't you, Nak.

Nak ignores the comment.

                    NAK (SUBTITLE)
                    (seriously)
          We've a long way to go.

                    SHIR (SUBTITLE)
                 (to Abdul)
           Don't worry; anything hunted will
           be killed and prepared Al Halal.
           Nak could wound a flea at a hundred
           feet if he had to.

The camels step off as Nak leads the way, a slow and steady
pace to be endured by all.

                                        DISSOLVE TO:

EXT. DESERT - MOMENTS LATER

LONG SHOT

The camel train is well clear of the ghantown, the last of
the buildings seen some distance behind it.

We see The vastness of desert and swing to the blistering sun
which then blinds the cinema screen.

EXT. DESERT - LATER

MONTAGE

Flies swarm around Nak's dry face. He waves them away after a
while, his face blank of expression.

Abdul slaps at a fly upon his face, a little sweat evident,
he looks around to stare at Shir who waves him a friendly
hello.

Shir's hand drops and he turns his head to check his camels.
Waves of glimmering heat continue rolling over the ground.

                                      SLOW FADE TO BLACK

EXT. CHAR ASIAB - DAWN (1879)

A shockingly loud gunshot fills the air.

Abdul has shot a Afghani soldier who was aiming directly at
him, but is hurled backwards himself as he is hit in the
chest.

Abdul has a wide smile upon his face. He then brings the
weapon down from his shoulder.

                    ABDUL (SUBTITLE)
           Praise be to Allah!

His smile then quickly evaporates. He feels somehow dirty for
what he has done.

Abdul continues with his advance upon the defensive position, the Afghans holding their ground rather well. The firing from the British guns now slows, it being too ineffective against the Afghans.

SMASH CUT TO

EXT. DESERT - AFTERNOON (THE PRESENT)

Abdul is brought back to the reality of the day.

Each of the cameleers speaks loudly in order to be heard, for distance between front and rear is large.

      NAK (SUBTITLE)
   Abdul... look, up ahead.

A figure can be seen up ahead of the camel string. Nak's lead camel is staring at the shape obscured by rolling waves of heat.

The string draws closer. It's an Aboriginal man, rather young, possibly 16, sitting beneath a bush. He becomes clearer. Nak feels a strong urge to turn away. The young man's face is scarred, his lips are burnt away completely. Abdul then sees the face, and he shudders at the sight and continues on. Shir has a quick look, too, and his smile disappears.

Another Aboriginal then comes to view towards the front of the camel train, a young half-caste child of five, his GRANDMOTHER behind him, very old and alone. She has a baby in her arms. Tears fill the grandmother's eyes. She speaks in Aboriginal.

     GRANDMOTHER (SUBTITLE)
   Please... please. I need some food
   for the children. Please... please;
   anything you have.

The woman holds her hand out.

    GRANDMOTHER (SUBTITLE) (CONT'D)
   A piece of jerky... some hard bread
   or a biscuit.

Nak pushes on. The string flows past the pleading woman. Some pots and pans from the kitchen camel towards the rear suddenly fall loose and commence clanging. The woman bursts out crying and the string continues on.

     ABDUL (SUBTITLE)
   Shouldn't we give some food?

                    NAK (SUBTITLE)
          She's Aborigine, more than
          competent enough to dig for her
          own, despite her age, and we've
          nothing to spare.

                    ABDUL (SUBTITLE)
          I've got some jerky.

Nak turns briefly to face Abdul. He then turns his back on
the man. All Abdul sees is Nak's back.

                    NAK (SUBTITLE) (O.C.)
          We've nothing!

We pull back to be confronted by the vastness of the desert.

                                        DISSOLVE TO:

EXT. DESERT - LATE AFTERNOON

The sun is approaching the horizon. Beautiful red and orange
streaks spread across the sky for as far as the eye can see.
Nak gives the call to halt. There's plenty of good spinifex
all around for the camels to feed upon.

                    NAK (SUBTITLE)
          We'll camp here for the night.
          Abdul... place the short hobbles
          onto your camels, I don't want them
          wondering too far on the first
          night.

Abdul waves acknowledgement.

SERIES OF SHOTS

Hobbles are set.

Loads are removed and placed beside their mounts.

The kitchen is moved over to where the camp fire will be
placed.

The sun hits the horizon and commences to disappear.

Prayer mats are placed upon the ground, small mounds of sand
beside them.

They each recite their prayers.

A final prayer is recited before the threesome tidy their
mats away.

END SERIES OF SHOTS

                              DISSOLVE TO:

EXT. DESERT - NIGHT

The stars are out in all their glory. A Meteor skips across
the night sky. Flames from the camp fire spit sparks into the
air. The three men drink their tea, a makeshift tent exists
in the background.

The fire illuminates the men's faces. Nak looks at Abdul and
sees that his forehead is furrowed.

                    NAK (SUBTITLE)
               You're wondering on the
               Aboriginals. You think I've been
               hard or unfair.

Abdul looks from Shir to Nak.

                    ABDUL (SUBTITLE)
               I would've thought there would've
               been more understanding.

                    SHIR (SUBTITLE)
               Give a little, they take a lot.
               Besides; we've nothing to give.

                    NAK (SUBTITLE)
               Thank you, Shir.

                    ABDUL (SUBTITLE)
               The boy had no lips.

                    NAK (SUBTITLE)
               I've heard many stories whilst in
               the desert.
                    (beat)
               Shall I tell you one?

                    ABDUL (SUBTITLE)
               It couldn't hurt; and I assume you
               have something to explain with this
               tale.

                    NAK (SUBTITLE)
               I'll let you be the judge of that.
                    (beat)
               There was an Aboriginal man. He
               looked down into the eyes of his
               new born girl... another mouth to
               feed, and of the wrong sex. That's
               what he thinks... the disgust upon
               his face tells the story.
                    (beat)
                         (MORE)

                    (CONT'D)
Anyhow, he picks her up by the feet
and bashes her hard against a rock,
her brains spilling out everywhere,
and right in front of the mother
and young son, a son whom is too
young and scarred to do a thing
about it.
          (beat)
Tears fall freely from the mother's
face. She has her arms held out...
she pleads... the man gives her a
back-hander. He then takes the body
of the new-born and moves down into
the creek line. He builds a fire
and places the body of the baby
girl into it, but the fire dies out
and the body remains.
          (beat)
A dingo then appears out of nowhere
and tears the body apart.

                    ABDUL (SUBTITLE)
I think I feel sick.

                    NAK (SUBTITLE)
You have to be human in order to be
sick.

                    ABDUL (SUBTITLE)
The man in the story was heinously
cruel... so very cruel.
          (beat)
But what does the story have to do
with what we saw... the boy with no
lips? What are you saying here,
Nak?

                    SHIR (SUBTITLE)
Nak has seen them before, had them
request food in the past.

                    ABDUL (SUBTITLE)
And?

                    NAK (SUBTITLE)
The old woman you saw, the one we
passed today. She's the mother of
the man in the story I just told,
but that was long ago; she acts now
as a guardian to her grandchildren.
Her son, the one who was so...
heinous, was not right in the head,
for he also took a stick from the
                    (MORE)

                    (CONT'D)
embers of a burning camp fire and
burnt away his son's lips, simply
because he wouldn't stop crying
when he was very young.

          ABDUL (SUBTITLE)
How can you be sure, Nak? How do
you know it to be true.

          NAK (SUBTITLE)
You know when someone's telling the
truth, it's written all over their
face. I've met many men in this
desert during my time here, and I
come to know the truth when I hear
it. I can guarantee the accuracy of
the story for I heard it direct
from a reliable source and wish to
say nothing more on the subject,
for some men don't deserve to be
accused of lies.

          ABDUL (SUBTITLE)
The family sounds as though they're
possessed by something evil.

          NAK (SUBTITLE)
It's more than that... it's simply
too devilish to comprehend. But the
Aboriginal woman stayed with the
the man. He passed from this world
several years ago.
     (beat)
You saw the baby that the old woman
had... the new child in her arms,
a half-cast, the result of laying
with a white man for a bottle of
drink.
     (beat)
Yes indeed, that's the way it is
here for some of them. The women
that was her daughter-in-law was
badly affected by the family
violence and come to know no
bounds. Desperate woman accept a
little coin from men, and man then
corrupts them... a little food, a
bottle of spirits... a few coins
which are good-for-nothing; any of
these and a man can have his way
with them.

Nak looks at Shir and then Abdul.

                    NAK (SUBTITLE) (CONT'D)
          They aren't all the same, most are
          reliable, strong and worthy even if
          misunderstood by the white-man, but
          the bad one's spoil it for the
          good.

There's a little silence now. Abdul yawns and stands up.

                    ABDUL (SUBTITLE)
          I'm tired. I'm sorry, my first day
          in the Australian desert has taken
          its toll on me. I've seen plenty of
          death in my time, but not
          disfigurement like what we saw
          today.

                    NAK (SUBTITLE)
          We'll both be joining you shortly,
          Abdul. Good night.

                    ABDUL (SUBTITLE)
          Good night, Nak... good night,
          Shir.

                    SHIR (SUBTITLE)
          Good night.

                                        DISSOLVE TO:

EXT. DESERT - SUNRISE

The sun has risen, prayers are over with.

The last of the camels are brought into line and seated into
position by Nak. Nak looks over briefly to the camp fire
where Shir and Abdul share breakfast; he cannot hear what
they are saying.

                    ABDUL (SUBTITLE)
          The desert's lonely, Shir? It's
          almost too much to bear, even after
          just a single day. At least when I
          was in Afghanistan there was always
          something to see and many comrades
          to share thoughts with.

                    SHIR (SUBTITLE)
          Try not to worry about it too much.
          I suffered, too, when I first
          arrived. And I know Nak has
          suffered. It's just a matter of
          getting used to it, and you will,
          in time.

Shir looks over to where Nak is finishing with his task
before looking again to Abdul.

                    SHIR (SUBTITLE) (CONT'D)
          But its more than the desert for
          Nak.
               (beat)
          He doesn't speak much of the
          infliction he has, but that scar
          and forced expression upon his face
          isn't his friend.

                    ABDUL (SUBTITLE)
          I feel sorry for him.
               (beat)
          And I feel so lonely without my
          wife.

                    SHIR (SUBTITLE)
          You'll get used to it all, and when
          you're in Marree you'll find that
          the support offered by everyone
          around is enough to help you
          progress from one day to the next.
          But believe me; you won't be
          spending too much time in Marree.
          From the day you arrived into our
          arms, as employee and friend, you
          said farewell to civilization. We
          support one another in he desert...
          now and for all time.

                    ABDUL (SUBTITLE)
          I miss my wife... my family.

                    SHIR (SUBTITLE)
          I understand... really, I do. We
          must all do what we have to do in
          order to survive. It's unfortunate
          that your sacrifice is more than
          what most must suffer in order to
          get ahead in life. But take my
          advice... try not to think of your
          wife. You won't survive if you keep
          thinking about her.

                    ABDUL (SUBTITLE)
          What else is there to think about
          when on the road for days on end,
          if not of family and friends?

                    SHIR (SUBTITLE)
          That's the hardest question to
          answer, everyone is different; we
                         (MORE

                     (CONT'D)
          each have a different mind. I can't
          answer your question, Abdul.

                     ABDUL (SUBTITLE)
          Then I'll find the answer for
          myself.

                     SHIR (SUBTITLE)
          And maybe that's the answer. Set
          your mind free of its shackles and
          cast your thoughts far and wide,
          but also... consider everything
          that's around you, look at every
          detail, take in all there is to
          learn. I can't tell you any more
          than that.

                     ABDUL (SUBTITLE)
          Thank you, Shir.

Abdul and Shir look up and see Nak approach the fire.

                     NAK (SUBTITLE)
                (with little emotion)
          Time to make a move. Let's be off.

                                             DISSOLVE TO:

EXT. DESERT - DAY

Nak sees a silhouette to his front, very far away and heading
in his direction.

BROTHER ERNEST JACOB is approaching slowly, a bullock team of
ten under his control, a wagon half full of supplies being
pulled easily along.

Each of the cameleers speaks loudly in order to be heard
whilst travelling, as is usual.

                     NAK (SUBTITLE)
          Bullock team!

Moments later.

                     NAK (SUBTITLE) (CONT'D)
          Missionary!

                     ABDUL (SUBTITLE)
          How can you be sure?

                     SHIR (SUBTITLE)
          Nak's always sure.

                    NAK (SUBTITLE)
          As they say in Marree: look and
          learn. The man's walking besides
          his team, a wagon pulled behind.

                    SHIR (SUBTITLE)
          Most Australians are too lazy to
          walk, Abdul. Most like to ride so
          that their arse is higher off the
          ground than ours.

Moments later.

                    NAK (SUBTITLE)
          It's the one they call, Brother
          Ernest Jacob. He prefers to walk.
          We see Jacob about one out of every
          five trips. He travels between
          Port Augusta and the mission at
          Killalpinanna.

                    SHIR (SUBTITLE)
          I guess he'll be thankful for the
          completed train track in Marree.
          He'll be able to move his supplies
          by transport from now on.

                    NAK (SUBTITLE)
          I don't know if he would.

                    SHIR (SUBTITLE)
          He'd be crazy not to.

                    NAK (SUBTITLE)
          Some of the Christians are just
          that.

                    ABDUL (SUBTITLE)
          What's at Killalpinanna?

                    NAK (SUBTITLE)
          Besides the mission? Nothing much.
          Just this stinking desert and more
          of the same.

Nak spits out a fly that lands in his mouth.

                    NAK (SUBTITLE) (CONT'D)
          Move to side!

Slowly the camel string moves aside to allow room for Jacob,
each camel following on, in contrast to the compartments of a
long train following a bend in the tracks.

                    NAK (SUBTITLE) (CONT'D)
          The mission is a day south of
          Cooper Creek. We'll bypass it.

                    ABDUL (SUBTITLE)
          Why's that, Nak.

                    NAK (SUBTITLE)
          The fewer whites we encounter, the
          better. It doesn't matter much
          where they come from. They're all
          the same. Unless we have supplies
          to deliver, we'll go around them.

Jacob is now upon them. Nak nods in friendly greeting.
Jacob speaks in German.

                    JACOB (SUBTITLE)
          May God be with you, brothers. Let
          him build an altar within you all,
          a church for which to heal your
          souls of the savagery embraced by
          your beliefs.

                    ABDUL (SUBTITLE)
          What did he say?

                    NAK (SUBTITLE)
          I've no idea. I don't understand a
          word.
                    (to Jacob)
          May Allah be with you.

Jacob is jolted by the name Allah, he scoffs and continues
ever on, a fake smile then returns to his lips. Abdul gives a
friendly nod as they pass, as does Shir.

                                        SLOW DISSOLVE TO:

EXT. COOPER CREEK - DAY

The team draws up just short of the creek, Nak turns to give
Abdul advise on the crossing. The camels are excited by the
smell of water.

                    NAK (SUBTITLE)
          Don't let your camels drink, Abdul.
          This isn't Afghanistan and we're
          not Australians. If the camels
          drink here then all of our good
          work with water discipline will be
          lost.

                    SHIR (SUBTITLE)
          Use your stick, Abdul... but use it
          sparingly.

                    NAK (SUBTITLE)
          Unless you like camels biting you
          on the arse.

The line of trees either side of the Cooper are home to many
birds; fishes and amphibian life thrives amongst the few
reeds, roots, and boulders. A frog jumps and disappears with
a splash.

The Afghans move slowly down towards the shallow and slowflowing
water.

                    NAK (SUBTITLE) (CONT'D)
          Think about it, Abdul. It's one of
          the reasons that the whites of this
          country use bullocks and horses
          instead of camels.
                    (beat)
          They're too damn lazy to teach
          their camels properly. They water
          their stock at every turn, at any
          opportunity. It's no wonder they
          can't get a good day's work out of
          a dromedary.

Shadows are cast upon the reflective surface of the creek and
come to life, dancing shades of color flickering upon the
surface of the Cooper.

                    NAK (SUBTITLE) (CONT'D)
          Come on... UP! UP!
                    (to Abdul)
          Ships-of-the-Desert; no need for
          water.

Nak produces his stick for the first time during the days
move. He hits out at the side of the third in line.

                    NAK (SUBTITLE) (CONT'D)
          UP! GET UP!
                    (beat)
          GET UP!
                    (to Abdul)
          Get that lazy bull... look, stop
          him!

Abdul strikes out at the camel to his front, hitting him in
the flank.

                    NAK (SUBTITLE) (CONT'D)
              Strike higher, Abdul, like this.

Nak races a few steps to the third in line and hits it, the
camel having bowed its head towards the water's surface. A
loud 'thwack' reaches Abdul's ears.

                    NAK (SUBTITLE) (CONT'D)
              My camels won't take the meaning of
              the discipline unless you strike
              them properly.

Abdul can't help but notice the cool looking water.

                    ABDUL (SUBTITLE)
              Looks like a good place to drink
              and pray.

                    NAK (SUBTITLE)
              We don't stop near water unless
              replenishing the team; it's unfair
              to the camels, and we don't pray at
              noon.

                    SHIR (SUBTITLE)
              This is our routine, Abdul. We
              don't change routine... it's too
              important for the camels and they
              always come first.

The old hands go into rhythm of verse.

                    NAK (SUBTITLE)
              Water is for the weak.

                    SHIR (SUBTITLE)
              And we are strong.

                    NAK (SUBTITLE)
              We will never break.

                    SHIR (SUBTITLE)
              For that would be wrong.

Abdul then strikes a camel trying to drink, it rears its head
when stung by the stick.

                    ABDUL (SUBTITLE)
              UP! GET UP!

                    NAK (SUBTITLE)
              Good work, Abdul.

                    SHIR (SUBTITLE)
          You're one of us, Abdul, an Afghan
          through and through.

The cameleers get wet, looking after the team. The saddle
packs and other stores sit high out of the water and remain
dry. Abdul cups his palm and draws water to his lips and
drinks. The water cascades down his chin and neck.

Within minutes the string is across the creek and the camels
are brought to a temporary stop.

                    NAK (SUBTITLE)
          Check your nose pegs, Abdul.

                    SHIR (SUBTITLE)
          Mine are all good.

Moments later.

                    ABDUL (SUBTITLE)
          Mine too; all good.

                    NAK (SUBTITLE)
          Good.
               (beat)
          And, Abdul... please don't let the
          camels see you drinking from the
          creek.

Nak turns away on giving the advice. He then sees something
up ahead.

The dark silhouette of a man upon a horse can be seen in the
distance. The dark shape watches the camel string for a
second before riding off in the opposite direction.

Abdul is drawn to Nak's stare and the silhouette.

                    ABDUL (SUBTITLE)
          What was that about?

                    NAK (SUBTITLE)
          Nothing... don't worry about it.
          Come on, let's get moving.

                                        DISSOLVE TO:

EXT. DESERT - DAY

SERIES OF SHOTS

The Natterannie Sandhills are ahead, yellow ridges filling
the scene before them. A wedge-tail eagle catches Abdul's eye
as it glides across the clear blue sky.

The Mungerannie Gap falls behind them, the open desert
offered them all.

Kangaroos cross their path, a lone emu, too.

AERIAL SHOT

An Aborigine can be seen wandering off into the distance.

END AERIAL SHOT

Clifton Hill station, remote and bare, comes to view from a
distance.

END SERIES OF SHOTS

                                        DISSOLVE TO:

EXT. CLIFTON HILL - DAY

Nak pulls the camel string to a halt.

Nak approaches Abdul to give him details on the short stop.

                    NAK (SUBTITLE)
          We will drop off the supplies and
          be on our way as soon as possible,
          Abdul, but we won't remain long...
          we still have a long way to go.
          There will be no need to talk to
          them... I'll tend to all of that.

                    ABDUL (SUBTITLE)
          It doesn't look like much is
          here... not much to see. I'm
          surprised we had no stores for
          Mulka.

                    NAK (SUBTITLE)
          We don't stop at Mulka, not unless
          due to sheer necessity, and usually
          bypass it as we have done.

                    ABDUL (SUBTITLE)
          I would have thought more business
          was available, it being more
          populated.

                    NAK (SUBTITLE)
          Forget it, Abdul. There's nothing
          to say about it. As for this place,
          your right; there isn't much here.
          It's currently owned by a mister
          Broad. He has himself over a
                    (MORE)

                    (CONT'D)
          thousand cattle in these parts.
          They're good enough people, but
          we're here to do a quick supply and
          nothing more. We don't have time
          for hospitality.

                    ABDUL (SUBTITLE)
          Okay, Nak.

SERIES OF SHOTS

Nak speaks with the headman.

Some stores are off-loaded.

Camels and saddles are checked.

They continue on their way.

END SERIES OF SHOTS

                                        DISSOLVE TO:

EXT. DESERT - LATE AFTERNOON

Nak sees a dingo up ahead, standing in the way of his
advance. It sniffs the air.

                    NAK (SUBTITLE)
          We've got a dingo up ahead and
          we're not long from preparing camp
          for the night, so keep your eyes
          open for more.

                    ABDUL (SUBTITLE)
          Will you shoot it.

The camel string is brought to a temporary halt and Nak takes
the rifle from its place upon the camel.

                    NAK (SUBTITLE)
          I'll make it wish it never crossed
          our path.

                    SHIR (SUBTITLE)
          You're about to see a true marksman
          at work, Abdul.

                    NAK (SUBTITLE)
          Quiet now.

Nak stands there for a moment with the rifle in his shoulder
and then lowers it.

                    NAK (SUBTITLE) (CONT'D)
               (a solemn look)
          No. I'll wait.
               (puts rifle away)
          Keep your eye on him.

                    ABDUL (SUBTITLE)
          You should shoot him now, Nak.

                    NAK (SUBTITLE)
          No; there looks to be only one. I
          don't want the camels breaking
          their nose pegs for one stinking
          dingo.

                    SHIR (SUBTITLE)
               (fails to hear)
          What was that?

                    ABDUL (SUBTITLE)
          Nak says we're to watch the dingo,
          see if it follows. He doesn't want
          the camels rattled.

                    SHIR (SUBTITLE)
          Maybe you should tell Nak something
          more.
               (beat)
          Slate's ready to give birth, and
          soon. I'd say we have about an hour
          at most.

                    NAK (SUBTITLE)
          I hear you.
               (pointing)
          We'll stop near that tree.

EXT. DESERT - DUSK

With prayers concluded, Nak puts away the Koran. He sees the
dingo. Nak reaches steadily for the rifle at his side. Abdul
notices his motion, Shir is tending Slate and the delivery of
the unborn.

Nak checks the sights and stands, taking up position next to
the tree. He aims and fires. The camels stir, two run off on
short hobbles.

The rifle is lowered.

                    SHIR (SUBTITLE)
          Well?

                    NAK (SUBTITLE)
          I missed.

> SHIR (SUBTITLE)
> Poor light.

> NAK (SUBTITLE)
> I told you, Shir... I've just been
> lucky in the past.

> SHIR (SUBTITLE)
> I don't believe you.

Nak sits back down at the fire.

> NAK (SUBTITLE)
> Abdul, keep an eye open for the
> dingo. It smells the birth.

> ABDUL (SUBTITLE)
> Of course.

Nak moves over to Shir who pats and strokes Slate.

> ABDUL (SUBTITLE) (CONT'D)
> Nak. He's turning back already.

> SHIR (SUBTITLE)
> He's courageous.

> NAK (SUBTITLE)
> He's a fool.

Nak stands and moves back to the tree and takes up the rifle.

He looks at the dingo.

> NAK (SUBTITLE) (CONT'D)
> Abdul. Here. You have a go.

> ABDUL (SUBTITLE)
> Me?

> NAK (SUBTITLE)
> Why not?

> ABDUL (SUBTITLE)
> Are you sure?

> NAK (SUBTITLE)
> Quickly, before he disappears again
> and comes crawling back when we're
> asleep.

Abdul takes up position and holds the rifle into his
shoulder. He aims and fires, the shot fills the air. The
dingo falls dead.

                    SHIR (SUBTITLE)
          Good shot, Abdul. Now, would
          someone like to give me a hand.
          It's coming... Slate's giving
          birth.

                    NAK (SUBTITLE)
          Another bastard of the bush.

                    ABDUL (SUBTITLE)
          Bastard of the bush?

                    NAK (SUBTITLE)
          Its how a white man expresses his
          hatred for something... anything.
          Doesn't matter if its dead or
          alive, be it a dingo or harmless,
          newborn calf.

                                        DISSOLVE TO:

EXT. DESERT - DUSK

Slate licks her newborn calf clean. There are smiles all
around. The other camels roam around on short hobbles but the
mother stays put. The calf suckles upon slate and Shir is
last to sit and enjoy the comfort of the fire.

                    NAK (SUBTITLE)
          Shir... She's your camel. Have
          something quick to eat and see to
          it.

Shir nods his head.

                    SHIR (SUBTITLE)
          I'll get the bag ready. I'll have
          Slate carry the kitchen, it'll be
          easier on her. Abdul... come and
          keep me company when you're ready;
          help me gather some grass.

Nak watches from beside the fire as Shir quickly grabs some
jerky, then he and Abdul begins to collect enough spinifex
and tussock grass to last the calf for the next two days.

                                        DISSOLVE TO:

EXT. CAMP FIRE - LATER

Nak hands Abdul and Shir a cup of tea as they sit beside the
fire.

                    NAK (SUBTITLE)
You've been working hard, Abdul.
How do you find it, here on the
road to Birdsville?

                    ABDUL (SUBTITLE)
It's like much of the rest of the
country, from what I've seen.

                    NAK (SUBTITLE)
Ah, well; it doesn't change much in
these parts, but the seasons bring
enough to provide your mind with a
little holiday from time to time.
Sometimes you can't move for the
land is flooded for miles around
and at others there'll be no rain
for many months on end, and water
can never be guaranteed.
        (beat)
We don't have wells here like in
Afghanistan, although I did hear of
a surveyor checking on the land
around Mungerannie Gap, a sure sign
that the government is thinking of
having them put in.

                    ABDUL (SUBTITLE)
You've experienced this; the
flooding and the drought?

                    NAK (SUBTITLE)
Both me and Shir.
        (beat)
Ah; it's hard work; and I've worked
hard for the entire time I've been
here.

                    ABDUL (SUBTITLE)
And you've yet to make your
fortune?
        (beat)
I'm sorry, I didn't wish to make it
sound like that.

                    NAK (SUBTITLE)
Like sarcasm? That's okay. Money's
hard to come by in Australia. It's
hard work being a cameleer. In
order for us to keep a job running
year in and year out we have to
keep prices low, too low to make a
real fortune, and life here is only
as comfortable as you make it. A
                    (MORE)

                    (CONT'D)
          little discomfort suffered in ones
          younger years is money in the bank,
          Abdul. It also favors the man who
          keeps many friends. But the only
          way to make a fortune is to save,
          and we save hard, don't we Shir?

                    SHIR (SUBTITLE)
          We do at that... and with double
          the discomfort.

                    ABDUL (SUBTITLE)
          Friends like Jehangir?

                    NAK (SUBTITLE)
          That's it, exactly. Good friends
          will help you, always. Jehangir was
          asked by me to look out for a
          strong young man as yourself,
          someone ready to move, someone with
          little baggage, someone to help me
          with the camels I have; and as good
          friends always do, he delivered.

                    ABDUL (SUBTITLE)
          You and Shir must've been working
          hard these past few years with so
          many camels between just the two of
          you.

                    NAK (SUBTITLE)
          No, no, no, no; not at all... We
          had another helping us but he met
          with an unfortunate... accident.

                    ABDUL (SUBTITLE)
          Oh. What happened?

EXT. DESERT - DAY

We see several frames of what Nak saw earlier at the Cooper
crossing; the dark silhouette on a horse; and return
immediately back to the scene.

EXT. CAMP FIRE - MOMENTS LATER

                    NAK (SUBTITLE)
          He was shot; I was going to tell
          you. Shot dead he was. That's no
          lie.
                    (beat)
          Listen to me, Abdul. There're very
          few that you can trust in this
                    (MORE)

                    (CONT'D)
          country, other than those that read
          from the Koran. Everywhere you turn
          you will be met by those wishing to
          see you dead. Why do you think we
          stray from the worn tracks, keeping
          clear of places like Mulka?

                    ABDUL (SUBTITLE)
          Tell me, Nak... I need to learn...
          I want to know.

                    NAK (SUBTITLE)
          The rifle I carry isn't just for
          food. It's also for self-defense.

                    ABDUL (SUBTITLE)
          Have you ever needed it; used it,
          against another person?

                    NAK (SUBTITLE)
          Never; not yet. But our friend, the
          one you replaced, his name was
          Muschky. He was a very good man,
          like yourself, with the ambition of
          becoming a great man, a great
          cameleer. Do you know that he had
          this idea in his head that he could
          become a business man, to work hand
          in hand with the miners of all
                    (MORE)

                    NAK (SUBTITLE) (CONT'D)
          description, and right across
          the face of this damned desert? He
          wanted nothing more than to meld
          with those of this country, to help
          them as best he could. He never had
          a sour word to say about anyone.

POV - NAK

We see a clear picture of MUSCHKY, 28 years old, both slender
and tall.

                    NAK (V.O.)(SUBTITLE)
          But one day, last year, and before
          spring fell upon us, we were on
          this very track and heading for
          home.

Muschky is second in line on the string of camels, and he is
smiling at something Nak has said, and Nak turns his head to
look at him.

                    NAK (V.O.)(SUBTITLE) (CONT'D)
          We were near Mulka when a shot was
          fired and Muschky dropped dead;
          shot in the head.

We see the bullet strike Muschky down.

END POV

                    ABDUL (SUBTITLE)
          That's no accident... that's
          murder. What happened next?

                    NAK (SUBTITLE)
          Nothing happened, Abdul. Nothing. I
          think the shot was meant to scare
          us but the shot ricochet off the
          supplies we were carrying and hit
          poor Muschky; but I can't be sure.
          Besides, what can two men do
          without a weapon to protect
          themselves?

                    ABDUL (SUBTITLE)
          You didn't have a rifle?

                    NAK (SUBTITLE)
          Not then, no.

                    ABDUL (SUBTITLE)
          So you never caught the murderer?

                    NAK (SUBTITLE)
          No. We'd little chance. We heard a
          horse in the far distance. We then
          heard others... they all rode off
          quickly.

                    ABDUL (SUBTITLE)
          So why are you telling me this now?

                    NAK (SUBTITLE)
          When you killed the dingo I was
          reminded of poor Muschky... I'm
          always reminded of him. I wanted to
          tell you once I got to know you
          better, but... It's too much for me
          to handle. I'm not very good with
          the rifle, and not very good at
          killing... not since Char Asiab.

EXT. THE PAST - MAIN STREET, MARREE - DAY

A recent memory is recalled by Abdul, which occurred near the
train station when they first met.

                    NAK (SUBTITLE)
          Are you Abdul Hassan?

                    ABDUL (SUBTITLE)
          Yes... I'm Abdul.

Abdul is staring at Nak. Nak subconsciously rubs at the scar
on his mouth and cheek with his left hand.

EXT. CAMP FIRE - LATER

                    ABDUL (SUBTITLE)
          You were in Char Asiab?

                    NAK (SUBTITLE)
          Yes. I fear the day that someone
          finds out about my actions against
          the British. But that's better than
          having betrayed my country.

                    ABDUL (SUBTITLE)
          You accuse me, Nak... of betrayal.

                    NAK (SUBTITLE)
          I'm sorry, Abdul; I didn't mean it
          like that, honestly.
               (beat)
          Abdul, you're our friend and
          friends speak openly. I know you
          believe you were justified in
          fighting alongside the British, as
          much as I believe in my quest
          against them, but now things are
          different. I've a life here and
          can't go back. If I'm found out
          then that'll be the end of me.
               (beat)
          I want you to carry the rifle,
          Abdul. You have the right to refuse
          but I'd like to see it in your
          hands.

                    ABDUL (SUBTITLE)
          No!

EXT. ABDUL'S AFGHAN HOME - DAY

We see several frames transpire during a short pause; Abdul's
wife and two children outside an adobe in Afghanistan. The
wife is milking a goat, the children, very young, are running
around.

EXT. - CAMP FIRE - MOMENTS LATER

                    ABDUL (SUBTITLE)
Maybe I fought with the British in
the past and know how to use a
weapon, but now... I have a family
to look after, to send money to.
You shouldn't hold any of this
against me. I want nothing to do
with your rifle.

                    NAK (SUBTITLE)
I hold nothing against you, Abdul.
But in defense of any action... if
I was to kill... it would be easier
for you to prove self-defense. I
can't chance that, in case I'm
found out.

                    ABDUL (SUBTITLE)
What of my safety?

                    NAK (SUBTITLE)
Abdul, I feel I've offended you
enough... I'm your friend, you must
believe me. I need you to
understand my position here, the
predicament that could have risen
if I did in fact have a weapon, and
did revenge poor Muschky's death.
     (beat)
You now know the story, you know
where I keep the rifle, and you're
clear in your mind of your position
in this society and of your ability
to prove self-defense. I've none of
that.

                    ABDUL (SUBTITLE)
You've all of those in Marree, your
friends. They respect you; they'd
help you.

                    NAK (SUBTITLE)
I've no family. I've my camels,
that's all.

                    SHIR (SUBTITLE)
It's for you to know everything,
Abdul. We don't wish to hide a
thing.

                    ABDUL (SUBTITLE)
And what about you, Shir? Why don't
you take the rifle and kill in
self-defense?

                                        SMASH CUT TO:

INT. AFGHAN HOME - NIGHT

We see into the past. Shir serves a British officer, his wife
and two children a meal.

                    SHIR (V.O.)(SUBTITLE)
          Because I'm a wanted man. That's
          right.

Shir cuts the man's throat in front of his two children.

                    SHIR (V.O.)(SUBTITLE) (CONT'D)
          I killed a white man before leaving
          Afghanistan.

Shir flees the scene. The children and wife are crying,
kneeling beside their husband and devoted father.

                    SHIR (V.O.)(SUBTITLE) (CONT'D)
          I'm wanted as a spy by the British.
          I could be treated poorly by judge
          and jury.

BACK TO SCENE

                    SHIR (SUBTITLE) (CONT'D)
          Yes, I see it in your eyes, the
          questions you have. No; that's the
          answer... you don't deserve to be
          surrendered to judge and jury any
          more than me, or Nak for that
          matter; but it's an execution that
          awaits us both if we're found out.
          But also... I feel something else.
          I feel as though I'd risk it all
          for a single shot at that infidel
          that killed poor Muschky, but I
          might falter in the kill, I might
          have second thoughts, and any delay
          in pulling the trigger could be the
          end of us all.
                    (beat)
          I didn't receive any great joy from
          killing the man in Afghanistan;
          that's the truth. I simply did my
          duty, as I saw it at the time. But
          time changes many things. I wish
          things were different, but it's too
          late for that now.

Abdul falls silent for a moment.

                    ABDUL (SUBTITLE)
          Do you think that killing a man
          would be any easier for me?

                    NAK (SUBTITLE)
          In self-defense... maybe.

                    ABDUL (SUBTITLE)
          I feel uneasy about all of this
          talk. What you've revealed to me
          this night...
                    (beat)
          Nak... Shir... your secrets are
          safe with me, but I won't carry the
          rifle.

                    NAK (SUBTITLE)
          That's fair.
                    (beat)
          But I'm still happy that you know
          the truth.

                    ABDUL (SUBTITLE)
          Yes, I now know.
                    (beat)
          Please, excuse me. I need to get
          some sleep now. Good night.

                    NAK (SUBTITLE)
          Good night, Abdul

                    SHIR (SUBTITLE)
          Good night, Abdul; sleep well.

                                        DISSOLVE TO:

EXT. CHAR ASIAB - DAY (1879)

British soldiers and Punjab Infantry continue their advance
upon the defensive position and Abdul returns to the killing,
preparing his weapon for firing once more.

Dust flies up from a long way off, out towards the flank, the
Punjab Cavalry being spurred on into the attack. Abdul hears
a distorted voice nearby.

                    VOICE (O.C) (SUBTITLE)
          It's time.

INT. TENT - SUNRISE

Abdul rubs his eyes.

                    SHIR (SUBTITLE)
          It's time, Abdul.

Abdul shakes the dream from his head and looks Shir in the
eye.

                    ABDUL (SUBTITLE)
          Thank you, Shir.

                    SHIR (SUBTITLE)
          Nak is up and about, gathering the
          camels. The two that were scared
          off can't be found.
                    (Beat)
          Come on, let's give him a hand and
          then have some breakfast.

EXT. TENT - CONTINUOUS

Abdul and then Shir exit the tent and see Nak approaching
from near the tree, the two lost camels now tethered. Abdul
is smiling, the white of his teeth can be seen as the sun
peaks the horizon.

                    ABDUL (SUBTITLE)
          Good morning, Nak. I see you've
          found yourself a handful.

They close the gap to meet Nak nearer where the other camels
are sitting, waiting to be loaded for the day ahead.

                    NAK (SUBTITLE)
          I wanted an early start.

                    ABDUL (SUBTITLE)
          Nak... I was thinking about last
          night.

                    NAK (SUBTITLE)
          No, Abdul... I apologize... I'm
          sorry.

                    ABDUL (SUBTITLE)
          There's no need to say that. We've
          to look to each other for comfort,
          we need to look to one another for
          support.
                    (beat)
          You know this country better than
          me, and I can see that I've a
          lot to learn.

                    SHIR (SUBTITLE)
          Shall we have breakfast?

                    ABDUL (SUBTITLE)
                    (laughing)
          Yes... I'm starving.

                                        DISSOLVE TO:

EXT. DESERT - DAY

SERIES OF SHOTS

The camel train continues on through the desert landscape.
The glimmering heat-wave is remorseless.

Kangaroos look up from feeding and stare at the camel train
as its passes them by.

END SERIES OF SHOTS

EXT. DESERT - LATE AFTERNOON

The new-born calf is tied tightly in its bag and sits upon
it's mother's back. The mother looks back to check on the
young one. The calf's head sticks out and sniffs Slate's ear.
Nak holds up his hand and points.

                    NAK (SUBTITLE)
          Shir... good spinifex and tussock
          ahead!

Shir looks and sees for himself, presenting a large knife in
order to cut some fodder for later.

                    NAK (SUBTITLE) (CONT'D)
               (to Abdul)
          Slate can be spared the task of
          searching for food tonight. You'll
          have to help by keeping your camels
          away from Slate's food supply.

                    ABDUL (SUBTITLE)
          I'll watch the entire string if you
          like, give you and Shir time to get
          the camp fire burning.

                    NAK (SUBTITLE)
          I'd appreciated that, Abdul...
          thank you.

EXT. DESERT - LATER

The fire is burning and the camels are wondering around on
short hobbles, Slate is eating her tussock and spinifex, her
calf is feeding. Abdul watches on from beside the fire.

                    ABDUL (SUBTITLE)
          It's so peaceful here.

Abdul looks up at the stars.

                    ABDUL (SUBTITLE) (CONT'D)
          I feel as though I'm truly at
          peace, here in the desert.

                    NAK (SUBTITLE)
Peace is a noble quality, squalor
is a peasants.

                    SHIR (SUBTITLE)
No, Nak... you're wrong. You don't
need nobility to feel at peace.

                    NAK (SUBTITLE)
Mmmm... maybe you're right, Shir.
     (to Abdul)
If you truly feel at peace, then
you're truly lucky.

                    ABDUL (SUBTITLE)
You must've had times in the past
when you felt at peace, felt the
true joy of life.

There's a brief silence.

                    NAK (SUBTITLE)
No, Abdul. Not since Char Asiab. I
cherish the work I did, and the
killing of the British soldiers was
a glorious thing at the time; but
not any more.
     (beat)
I feel as though I'm a thief, a
cheater, having cheated men of
life.

                    SHIR (SUBTITLE)
Like the bastards that cheated poor
old muschky.

                    NAK (SUBTITLE)
They might be Christians and
Catholics.. and to tell you the
truth I don't know the difference.

                    SHIR (SUBTITLE)
And why should you?

                    NAK (SUBTITLE)
But I've taken the life from men
and displayed great pleasure in
doing so.
     (beat)
But look at the scar upon my face.
It's a constant reminder... it's
punishment for what I've done.

                    ABDUL (SUBTITLE)
What you did you did for Allah.

                    NAK (SUBTITLE)
          What I did was wrong.
                    (looking to Abdul)
          I can't kill again. I'm empty.

Abdul stands up from the fire and walks over to their
equipment. Nak and Shir watch on. Abdul takes the rifle from
Nak's possessions and carries to his own gear and places it
away. He returns to the fire.

                    ABDUL (SUBTITLE)
          The burden's mine now.

                    NAK (SUBTITLE)
          Thank you, Abdul.

Shir slaps Abdul on the shoulder.

                    SHIR (SUBTITLE)
          We're as one, Abdul. We'll never
          forget this day.

Everyone is smiling and nodding.

                    NAK (SUBTITLE)
          This is a great friendship we
          have... and tomorrow we'll be at
          the homestead. I've got some news
          I've been keeping from you; good
          news.

                    SHIR (SUBTITLE)
          Tell us, Nak.

                    NAK (SUBTITLE)
          We might be able to get a contract
          with the Diamantina police station.

                    SHIR (SUBTITLE)
          A good job indeed, two birds with a
          single stone.

                    ABDUL (SUBTITLE)
          Why's that?

                    SHIR (SUBTITLE)
          It's not far from the homestead
          that we'll be arriving at
          tomorrow.

                    NAK (SUBTITLE)
          I'll need more camels.

                    SHIR (SUBTITLE)
An extra hand to help with the
string.

                    ABDUL (SUBTITLE)
Sounds promising.

                    NAK (SUBTITLE)
It does. I know a man in Marree
that might be able to help us out
with a good purchase of
dromedaries.

                    SHIR (SUBTITLE)
We've got a few days to spare once
we get back to Marree. Do what you
can, Nak.

Abdul has a drink of his tea.

                    NAK (SUBTITLE)
We'll be okay if both Abdul Wade
and Faiz Mahomet stay out of our
face. The man I know said that the
information he attained came from a
young woman... apparently young and
very beautiful.

                    ABDUL (SUBTITLE)
It's amazing, the power that a
woman has.

                    NAK (SUBTITLE)
And Shir can attest to that.

                    SHIR (SUBTITLE)
Ah, yes... to think that I'm now a
married man.

                    NAK (SUBTITLE)
Ah, ha... I see it in your eyes.
You'd forgotten all about her,
hadn't you? Thinking more and more
about that pesky camel of yours:
Slate and her calf.

                    SHIR (SUBTITLE)
I'm hurt. To say that I feel more
for a camel than I do my own
wife... it's utterly absurd.

                    NAK (SUBTITLE)
You're amongst friends now, Shir.
Tell us the truth. What do you
say, Abdul?

                    ABDUL (SUBTITLE)
          I, ah... well; to be quite honest I
          think Shir has been rather taken in
          by the delivery of his calf.

                    SHIR (SUBTITLE)
          I'm utterly disgusted by you both
          for thinking so unkindly of my
          attraction to Slate... I mean, my
          wife.

                    NAK (SUBTITLE)
          Ah, ha; there you have it. You feel
          more for your damned camels than
          you do your own wife; and that
          proves it.

                    SHIR (SUBTITLE)
          Well... a camel can't do the things
          that a wife can do.

                    NAK (SUBTITLE)
          That depends on the cameleer that
          you talk to.

All three men burst into laughter.

                                        DISSOLVE TO:

EXT. DESERT - DAWN

All three men are awake and at work as the sun commences to
rise above the horizon.

The last camel is brought into line, the bell around its neck
ringing, saddle packs lined out ready to be loaded. The bull
in Abdul's care is blowing his bladder out.

                    ABDUL (SUBTITLE)
          This one's been blowing hard all
          the way back in.

Nak is half bent over looking at the feet of another camel
and can't see directly.

                    NAK (SUBTITLE)
          Which one?

                    ABDUL (SUBTITLE)
          Joy.

Nak looks up and over to where Abdul is standing.

                    NAK (SUBTITLE)
          Yes... that's Joy alright. You'll
          have to keep him away from the
          folks at the homestead... they'll
          not appreciate the smell.

                    ABDUL (SUBTITLE)
          You never told me their names.

                    NAK (SUBTITLE)
          The man's name is Alfred and his
          wife, she's crazy.

                    ABDUL (SUBTITLE)
          Crazy; that sounds like a funny
          name for a woman.

                    NAK (SUBTITLE)
               (seriously)
          No... I mean she's simply crazy.
          Her names Marge, but you have to
          call her Mrs Stapleton... if at
          all.

                    ABDUL (SUBTITLE)
          Funny name for a bull, too.

                    NAK (SUBTITLE)
          Joy is joy, male or female. It
          doesn't matter which.

                    ABDUL (SUBTITLE)
          It might if you were a camel.

                    NAK (SUBTITLE)
               (dryly)
          That's not funny, Abdul.

                    SHIR (SUBTITLE)
          That's okay, Abdul. Don't mind Nak.
          He's usually this way on the
          morning we face a homestead. They
          can be really nasty to deal with.

Nak stands erect and stretches.

                    NAK (SUBTITLE)
          With any luck we'll be at the
          homestead before noon.
               (beat)
          Come on, let's get going.

                                        DISSOLVE TO:

EXT. HOMESTEAD - DAY

The homestead is not far ahead, a wooden house, shed and
storage shelter coming to view. We can see a shearing shed
and a small windmill that pumps water from a borehole.
Several eucalyptus trees line a dry creek bed and troths lay
empty near the water pump. The farmer exits his house and
steps down from the veranda, brushing his hands against his
thighs.

The string of camels is halted and Nak stands there awaiting
the farmer to close the gap. ALFRED gives a nod of his head.
His wife, MARGE, comes out to watch from the veranda.

Alfred removes his hat, wipes his brow and returns the hat
upon his head.

                    NAK
               (to alfred)
          So... wool ready. Where?

Alfred licks his lips and approaches.

                    ALFRED
          Look. You see. Over there beside
          the house. You take; you take
          and put on camel after unload. You
          see?

Nak sees contempt in Alfred's eyes.

                    NAK
          Where unload?

Alfred is agitated.

                    ALFRED
          Over there, in the shed, alongside
          the wool. The same place as last
          time you were here.

                    NAK
          You lucky, no vermin.

                    ALFRED
          No, what?

                    NAK
          No rat... you no rat.

                    ALFRED
          Ah... mice; yes, plenty rat.
               (flustered)
          There are rats right across this
          bloody country. What do you think;
          we don't have rats up here?

                    NAK
          Unload on ground, yes?

Alfred raises his voice slightly.

                    ALFRED
          No! Same as last time... off
          ground, up... away from wet. Wet
          season come soon.

                    NAK
          Okay, I work now.

Nak turns to the others

                    NAK (SUBTITLE) (CONT'D)
          He wants the stores unloaded in the
          shed. Shir, see to it that the
          calf is watered immediately and
          I'll start with the unloading...
          you're with me, Abdul.
               (beat)
          Let's get this job done.

The camels are distressed, waiting to be watered, some
chewing a little cud as the unloading is commenced.

Alfred moves over to the troughs and pulls a chain near the
tank and the water starts to flow.

Albert's wife approaches one particular package that is
wrapped in red cloth. She turns to ensure that her only child
of three years is safe and out of harm's way.

                    MARGE
          Stay there, sweetheart... don't
          come near the dirty camels. They
          smell, darling.

Shir watches as Marge tends the article in red. He sees Nak
busy with unloading and the farmer pointing over to the bails
of wool.

Shir then looks back to Marge and the article is unwrapped.
There before his very eyes, thirty feet away, is a stack of
salted bacon slivers.

                    SHIR (SUBTITLE)
          Nak... NAK!

                    NAK (SUBTITLE)
          What is it, Shir?

                    SHIR (SUBTITLE)
          There, the woman.
               (pointing)
          Bacon... we've been transporting
          bacon.

Nak stomps over to Alfred, infuriated.

                    NAK
          What this!

The farmer sees what the matter is.

                    ALFRED
          Wait... Sorry, me sorry.

                    NAK
          You damn man. You very bad.

                    ALFRED
          No, look... you watch; please!

With great fury in his face, lips tight, creases forming upon
the skin around his eyes and cheeks, Alfred steps briskly
over to his wife and slaps her hard across the face. She
falls to the ground along with the bacon.

Marge bursts out sobbing, rubbing her cheek, reaching for the
bacon as it lays upon the ground.

Alfred kicks the bacon out of reach.

                    ALFRED (CONT'D)
          You stupid bitch!

Alfred looks to Nak in apology and speaks hurriedly.

                    ALFRED (CONT'D)
          My wife is so ridiculously stupid;
          I didn't know about the bacon. It's
          finished with now, yes?

                    NAK
          No! No more work. You get bullock
          fetch wool. We go, is finished.

          ALFRED
          No, wait, please. I didn't know
          about the bacon, I swear it. If I'd
          know about it I would've stopped it
          in Marree. This should never have
          happened, you must understand.
               (he slows his speech)
          I pay more, little extra. Pay for
                    (MORE)

                    (CONT'D)
          five more days on road, you get
          extra money, you get pay at post
          office in Marree.
                    (beat)
          Look, I write letter, give you; you
          take. You give post office and he
          pay much... you understand? You
          give letter to John Arthur
          O'Brien.

                    NAK
                    (hesitates)
          Bacon is bad.

                    ALFRED
          No more bacon, never any more, all
          finished... never see again.

                    NAK
          Okay. We do... job, for you. We
          water camel and load wool; we go
          Marree.

                    ALFRED
          Oh, Thank you, thank you.

                    SHIR (SUBTITLE)
          Ask for more money on top of what
          he might offer. Take from him what
          means the most.

                    NAK (SUBTITLE)
          No. I won't become one of them.

                    NAK (CONT'D)
                    (to Alfred)
          We do job, is okay... bacon
          finished.

                    ALFRED
          Yes, yes... is finished.

Alfred reaches out and shakes hands with Nak. Nak then
reaches in and produces two letters for Alfred.

                    NAK
          For you, from Marree... O'Brien.

Alfred reads the letters as the work continues.

Alfred smiles, Marge wipes tears from her eyes as she's
comforted by her daughter upon the veranda, and Nak joins the
others.

                                        DISSOLVE TO:

EXT. HOMESTEAD - AFTERNOON

The wool is finally loaded, 2 large bails per camel. The
string of camels departs the homestead.

LONG SHOT

The string moves away and the farmer and his wife can be seen
upon the veranda. Shir takes one last look before returning
his attention back to his work.

                                              DISSOLVE TO:

EXT. WATERHOLE - AFTERNOON

A waterhole is approached just off the main track, a
billabong with plenty of shade, reeds, and wildlife. A water
fowl takes flight. The string comes to a halt.

                    NAK (SUBTITLE)
          Let the camels finish watering.
          Fill your canteens if they need it.

                    ABDUL (SUBTITLE)
          This is a beautiful spot, Nak. Why
          don't we stay here the night?

                    NAK (SUBTITLE)
          Because we still have an hour of
          daylight left.

                    ABDUL (SUBTITLE)
          Are you okay, Nak? You sound upset.

                    NAK (SUBTITLE)
          Those damn farmers are all the
          same, Abdul... bastards one and
          all.

The remainder of the watering takes little time and is done
in silence. The caravan continues on after only nine of the
camels choose to take more water.

EXT. DESERT - EVENING

The camp is erected and the fire is prepared. the camels in
the background search for food, restricted by short hobbles.

                    NAK (SUBTITLE)
          Abdul... get some more fire wood,
          will you?

                    ABDUL (SUBTITLE)
          Sure.

Abdul moves over to a large portion of trunk and leans over
to pick it up. The wood is shifted and a scorpion is
disturbed. Abdul gets stung on the index finger of his right
hand.

                    ABDUL (SUBTITLE) (CONT'D)
          Ahhh! damn.

                    NAK (SUBTITLE)
          What is it, Abdul?

Nak and Shir race to his aid.

                    NAK (SUBTITLE) (CONT'D)
          I'm not sure... There, there it is.
               (beat)
          Damn it, a scorpion.

Abdul cradles his arm to his chest. He pulls the hand away
and looks at the wound as Shir and Nak appear at his side.

                    NAK (SUBTITLE) (CONT'D)
          Let me see.
               (beat)
          You're young, Abdul, and the
          Australian scorpion is rarely
          deadly, if at all.
               (to Shir)
          Isn't that right?

                    SHIR (SUBTITLE)
          Yes, that's right, Abdul. You're a
          strong man.

                    ABDUL (SUBTITLE)
          The pain is starting to build
          already.

                    SHIR (SUBTITLE)
          It's very red.

                    NAK (SUBTITLE)
          This is the first scorpion bite
          I've ever seen.

                    ABDUL (SUBTITLE)
          It's starting to throb now.

                    NAK (SUBTITLE)
          There's not much we can do I'm
          afraid. I honestly can't recall
          anyone being killed from a scorpion
          bite.

                    SHIR (SUBTITLE)
          I heard of a child once.

                    NAK (SUBTITLE)
          A child isn't a man.

Nak looks purposely into Abdul's eyes.

                    NAK (SUBTITLE) (CONT'D)
          You're a strong man, Abdul.

                    ABDUL (SUBTITLE)
          So I've heard already.
               (beat)
          How long will the pain last?

                    NAK (SUBTITLE)
          Maybe tomorrow you'll feel
          better... I'm sure it won't last
          long.

                    ABDUL (SUBTITLE)
          I won't sleep well like this. I
          don't wish to shy from my
          responsibilities.

                    NAK (SUBTITLE)
          Forget it, Abdul. Shir and I will
          do the work. Look, We'll get you
          something to eat and drink and
          then... we'll see how things go
          tonight. Tomorrow is a new day.

                    SHIR (SUBTITLE)
          I'll lay your prayer mat out,
          Abdul.

                    ABDUL (SUBTITLE)
          Thank you, Shir. Thank you both.

                                        DISSOLVE TO:

EXT. DESERT - DAY

The camels are moving along nicely. Nak looks over his
shoulder to see Abdul in seemingly good stride and turns
again to face the front.

Abdul's face is displaying a lot more pain now than the night
before. A little bead of sweat appears upon his forehead. He
suddenly stumbles over his own feet but manages to prevent
himself from falling, his face wincing as his arm is jarred.

                    SHIR (SUBTITLE)
          Are you okay, Abdul?

Abdul half turns his head to reply.

                    ABDUL (SUBTITLE)
          Yes; thank you.

Nak turns once more as the camel string continues on.

                    NAK (SUBTITLE)
          How's the finger now?

                    ABDUL (SUBTITLE)
          It's getting worse.

                    NAK (SUBTITLE)
          Do you need to stop and rest.

                    ABDUL (SUBTITLE)
          No. Let's keep moving; don't stop.

                    SHIR (SUBTITLE)
          You're a good man, Abdul. The work
          will take your mind off the sting.

There's a monstrous sandstorm in the background.

Nak pulls the string to a halt. We see Nak's jaw drop
slightly.

                    SHIR (SUBTITLE) (O.C.)
          What is it, Nak... What's wrong?

Nak points into the distance.

The others look to see for themselves the horror of the
situation.

From North to South, across the entire expanse of the sky is
a darkened mass of billowing red sand. It is rolling towards
them at great speed, like a giant wave surging towards them.

                    NAK (SUBTITLE)
          Quickly, Shir, get the shelter from
          the pack, put it up over there next
          to the mulga tree. Abdul, get the
          water and some biscuits from the
          kitchen, we don't have much time;
          quickly now.

The men rush to attend to their tasks. Nak manages to get the
calf free from Slates back. The makeshift tent is erected in
hast, a single rope securing it to the tree.

Nak cuts the lines on the camel string. Shir looks up.

>   SHIR (SUBTITLE)
>   What are you doing, Nak?

>   NAK (SUBTITLE)
>   The camels will be better off this
>   way. Come on, get the tent
>   finished.

>   SHIR (SUBTITLE)
>   We don't have time, look.

Nak turns to see the sandstorm almost upon them.

>   NAK (SUBTITLE)
>   Hurry up, Abdul, quickly now.

>   SHIR (SUBTITLE)
>   Nak! Tie the calf to Slate, keep
>   them together.

>   NAK (SUBTITLE)
>   It's too late, get into cover, now!

>   ABDUL (SUBTITLE)
>   I'll do it.

>   NAK (SUBTITLE)
>   No, Abdul!

Abdul freezes for a split second and then does as Shir has
requested, placing a cord between the mother and the sibling.
Nak rushes back to the tent with some biscuits and water,
Shir quickly dragging blankets into the shallow tent. Then
panic hits him.

>   SHIR (SUBTITLE)
>   Nak! The koran! We need it!

>   NAK (SUBTITLE)
>   I'll get it, you get into the tent,
>   now!

Nak scrambles for the Koran on the camel, the camel bolts
several yards further away. The sandstorm suddenly hits hard
and Nak is engulfed in misery.

INT. TENT CANVAS - CONTINUOUS

The whistling thunder of noise is deafening, the tent is
flapping vigorously, slapping against Shir and Abdul. The
interior is now much darker than before.

EXT. TENT CANVAS - CONTINUOUS

Nak feels a camel's body and then neck. The camel sits down
its wool still upon its back. Nak pulls out his knife and
cuts the thongs, dropping his knife as he tries to put it
back into its sheaf. Nak can barely see a thing. The noise is
deafening.

Nak feels the koran and pulls it from its place and falls to
his knees. He scrambles away towards the tent as best he can.
He's crawling now. He doesn't make it to the tent.

INT. TENT CANVAS - CONTINUOUS

The ferocity of the storm is unbelievable.

                    SHIR (SUBTITLE)
          Abdul! Are you okay?

                    ABDUL (SUBTITLE)
          What?

Shir holds onto Abdul's good arm.

                    SHIR (SUBTITLE)
          Are you okay!

Abdul nods his head.

                    ABDUL (SUBTITLE)
          Where's Nak?

                    SHIR (SUBTITLE)
          What?

                    ABDUL (SUBTITLE)
          Do you think something has happened
          to Nak?

                    SHIR (SUBTITLE)
          No... But there's nothing we can do
          anyway!

EXT. TENT CANVAS - CONTINUOUS

Nak continues to crawl, the koran in his grasp. He finds
shelter on the reverse side of a rock and proceeds no
further. He collapses and becomes buried, pelted by the
grains of sand.

We close in on Nak and can see momentarily into his mind.

                                        DISSOLVE TO:

EXT. CHAR ASIAB - DAY (1879)

The British are advancing rapidly against the Afghan position

and Nak fires his rifle one more time. He lifts his head to
see better, looking into the low ground.

A member of the Punjab Infantry suddenly appears some forty
feet before him and fires a shot. The lead hits Nak square in
the mouth, ripping his lips and cheek apart. Nak falls down
for a few seconds but manages to get to his feet. He now
climbs from the defenses and runs alongside others making
good their escape, blood smeared all over him.

EXT. TENT CANVAS - LATER

Nak is being covered in sand, the storm growing in ferocity.
Nak brings his hand up to his face and attempts to open his
eyes but the storm is too fierce. He cowers against the
shelter of the rock.

INT. TENT - CONTINUOUS

The ferocity of the storm sees the tent thrash Abdul and Shir
without remorse. They fight to sit upon the bottom edge of
the tent and then push backwards in order to make enough
space for them to see each other, their backs against the
coarse material which shelters them from the storm.

The fabric of the tent folds around their bodies, but a
little breathing space is attained.

They look into each others eyes as best they can, the
darkness within making it hard to see. Shir fumbles with some
biscuits and lays these between them, Abdul does the same
with some water.

They commence to pray silently to themselves, rocking gently
to their verses, mouths moving.

DISSOLVE TO:

INT. TENT CANVAS - LATER

Shir reaches for the biscuits and opens them up. He hands
Abdul his share.

Abdul nods thanks. They eat. Abdul opens the water container
and takes a drink, offering some to Shir who also drinks.
They continue to sit in silence.

We pull back through the fabric of the tent.

EXT. TENT CANVAS - CONTINUOUS

The storm outside continues, the dark of the storm hiding the
fact that day has passed into night. We pull back from the
storm and see the stars above.

EXT. TENT CANVAS - MOMENTS LATER

Nak is laying very still, the sand piling up around him. He shifts slightly. He pushes closer to the rock and there he remains.

DISSOLVE TO:

INT. TENT CANVAS - VERY EARLY MORNING

The storm continues. Shir stirs and sits up after a little sleep. He checks the biscuits and takes two out. He eats and then takes a drink. He looks at Abdul and pushes the biscuits towards his sleeping form.

Abdul wakes then and sits up too. Shir points to the biscuits and Abdul tempts a smile. He reaches for the biscuits but quickly pulls his hand back in pain. His finger is worst than before. Shir takes several biscuits and places them into Abdul's good hand. He eats.

EXT. TENT CANVAS - MOMENTS LATER

The camels outside are sitting, the sand piling up about them. Loose equipment is being dispersed across the desert landscape.

DISSOLVE TO:

INT. TENT CANVAS - SUNRISE

The wind seems to be abating. Shir is awake, Abdul is asleep. Abdul's face fills the screen. His eyeballs are erratic beneath eyelids. Abdul is dreaming.

EXT. CHAR ASIAB - DAY

Abdul is fighting forward, a part of the British line, a part of the Punjab Infantry. He points his rifle and pulls the trigger. We follow the shot and it smacks Nak in the mouth. Moments later Abdul is racing towards the defensive position, comrades either side of him, the cavalry approaching fast. Abdul looks forward and sees a man stand. He sees Nak as plain as day. He's shot Nak in the face. An explosion occurs nearby and Nak takes cover.

SMASH CUT TO:

INT. TENT CANVAS - CONTINUOUS

The explosion echoes and dissipates as Abdul's eyes flash open, we can hear his heart racing. The heart beating subsides and Shir can be heard.

                    SHIR (SUBTITLE)
          Abdul... Abdul... are you okay?

                    ABDUL (SUBTITLE)
          Yes... yes, I'm alright!

                    SHIR (SUBTITLE)
          The wind is slowing. I think it's
          morning.

Abdul looks at his finger, pain written all over his face.

                    SHIR (SUBTITLE) (CONT'D)
          How's your finger?

                    ABDUL (SUBTITLE)
          It's not good.

                    SHIR (SUBTITLE)
          I think you had a bad dream.

                    ABDUL (SUBTITLE)
          Yes, I did.
               (beat)
          I hope Nak's alright.

                    SHIR (SUBTITLE)
          We'll have to have a look for him
          once the storm clears, but at the
          moment there's not much we can do.
               (beat)
          Let me see your finger.

                    ABDUL (SUBTITLE)
          It hurts like hell. What time do
          you think it is.

                    SHIR (SUBTITLE)
          Way past morning prayer. The wind
          is still too strong to take a look
          outside. We'll have to wait.

                    ABDUL (SUBTITLE)
          I think we should try. I have to do
          something about my finger. We have
          to find Nak.

Shir considers Abdul.

                    SHIR (SUBTITLE)
          What do you want to do, Abdul? Can
          I help?

                    ABDUL (SUBTITLE)
          I think it needs to be removed.

                    SHIR (SUBTITLE)
          Please, Abdul... wait. We've no
          biscuits left and only a little
          water. We should stay put. You
          should try and get some more sleep.

                    ABDUL (SUBTITLE)
          I can't, it hurts too much.

                    SHIR (SUBTITLE)
          You'll have to try... please.

Abdul nods his head and slowly but surely they both lay their
heads back down.

                                        DISSOLVE TO:

INT. TENT CANVAS - EVENING

Shir wakes suddenly, the shocking weight of the sand pushing
upon him from outside the tent. He sees Abdul sitting up,
rocking cross-legged, holding his finger, tears upon his
cheek.

Shir pushes to sit up.

                    SHIR (SUBTITLE)
          Let me see.

Abdul reluctantly shows his finger to his friend. Shir feels
his pain. The finger is huge and discolored. Suddenly the
wind dies down, gone as quickly as it came.

Shir looks at Abdul and exits the tent. He turns there,
halfway out.

                    SHIR (SUBTITLE) (CONT'D)
          It's over with, Abdul. The storm
          has stopped.

Shir scrambles out and folds the tent up and over Abdul,
dispersing the sand. Shir pushes it aside.

Abdul continues to cradle his hand as Shir looks around for
any sign of Nak and the camels. A few heaps of sand can be
seen and the first of the camels stir.

Half of them have not moved but others have wandered off.

Equipment is strewn all over the immediate area, the heaviest
not far from where the camels were initially seated.

The sun comes out from hiding, but the night is approaching
fast, less than 30 minutes of light remaining. Shir looks to
the rear of the vanishing storm and then looks to where the

remaining camels were last known to be.

Piles of sand indicate where some camels sit. Shir races over to them. He scrambles to move the sand from one small and one large pile. Slate and her calf are dead. Two others are seen as they stand up.

> ABDUL (SUBTITLE)
> I'm sorry, Shir. It's not fair.

Shir turns abruptly and sees Abdul is in much pain. Shir then looks left and right.

> SHIR (SUBTITLE)
> Nak! Nak! Where are you?

Nak stands up from behind the rock, looking worst for wear, the koran open in his hand.

His lips are cracked; his face is covered in sand.

> NAK (SUBTITLE)
> Here! I'm over here!

Nak closes the koran and starts to walk over but stops. He hears a bell. He sees a camel and moves over to it.

> NAK (SUBTITLE) (CONT'D)
> Look for the camels, quickly.

> SHIR (SUBTITLE)
> I have to see to Abdul.

Nak sees Abdul in pain and moves to him. The three are now together. Nak looks at Shir.

> NAK (SUBTITLE)
> Forget the camels for the moment,
> this is more important. Get the
> fire going, Shir.

Abdul manages a small smile.

> DISSOLVE TO:

EXT. TENT - LATER

They sit around the camp fire and look around at each other, the now erected tent just behind them.

Gathered camels can be seen resting.

> ABDUL (SUBTITLE)
> It's almost dark. I think its time
> to do something about my finger.

                NAK (SUBTITLE)
What can we do? There's nothing.

                ABDUL (SUBTITLE)
It needs to be amputated.

                NAK (SUBTITLE)
Are you mad?

                SHIR (SUBTITLE)
He's right, Nak... Something needs
to be done.

                ABDUL (SUBTITLE)
It has to be done, Nak. I can't
move my arm, the pain's unbearable.
If something isn't done soon, I'm
going to die .

                NAK (SUBTITLE)
What's cutting your finger off
going to do?

                ABDUL (SUBTITLE)
It'll take away the source of the
pain.

                NAK (SUBTITLE)
The source of your pain is your
arm... should we amputate that?

                SHIR (SUBTITLE)
Be fair, Nak.

                ABDUL (SUBTITLE)
I hope not, but if it must be done,
then it must be done. I don't care
about my arm now. Something has to
be done and quickly. My entire arm
is killing me, but the source of
the pain is my finger... that's
where I was stung.

                SHIR (SUBTITLE)
He's right. He should take off the
finger. I've shared a lot with
Abdul whilst in the tent and I
recall, quite distinctly, that a
man of Afghanistan, near my village
in fact, took off his finger under
similar circumstances.

                ABDUL (SUBTITLE)
I've heard a similar story.

                    NAK (SUBTITLE)
          We've all 'heard'. That story's
          very old and has been told many
          times. Much has been forgotten in
          its passing from one to another.
          You can never rely on fables.

                    ABDUL (SUBTITLE)
          Nak, look at me... look into my
          eyes.

Nak rubs the scar upon his face. He feels the pain.

                    NAK (SUBTITLE)
          Okay... I'll do it. I'm the
          jemadar, it'll be my
          responsibility.

                    ABDUL (SUBTITLE)
          Thank you, Nak; but please hurry.

                    NAK (SUBTITLE)
          Shir, get the clippers from my
          saddle bag... and a small rock;
          I've lost my knife.

Shir does as asked, Nak looks at the wound. Nak pulls a large
rock closer.

                    NAK (SUBTITLE) (CONT'D)
          Put your hand down here, Abdul.

Nak can see Shir coming back with the items in his hands.

                    SHIR (SUBTITLE)
          Will these do?

                    NAK (SUBTITLE)
          That's fine. Come here.
               (beat)
          Thanks, Shir.

Nak opens the clippers so that they resemble a cross. He
holds the sharp edge of one of the cross sections above the
knuckle of Abdul's finger.

                    NAK (SUBTITLE) (CONT'D)
          I'm going to hit the clippers with
          the rock, Abdul. I'll do it hard
          and fast, as hard as I possibly
          can.

                    ABDUL (SUBTITLE)
          Please hurry.

                    NAK (SUBTITLE)
          It's going to hurt. It probably
          won't feel any better for quite
          some time.

                    ABDUL (SUBTITLE)
          Please.

                    NAK (SUBTITLE)
          Are you—.

                    ABDUL (SUBTITLE)
          Now, Nak! QUICKLY!

                    NAK (SUBTITLE)
          Look away, Abdul, so you don't
          flinch. Get ready with the bandage,
          Shir.

Before Shir can give an answer the finger is lobbed off, cut
clean away.

The pain is great, Abdul rolls upon the ground momentarily
and then forces himself to sit as he restrains himself. Nak
drops his tools and give aid to Abdul. Shir places the
bandage around Abdul's hand and small stump.

                    NAK (SUBTITLE) (CONT'D)
          That must have hurt.

                    ABDUL (SUBTITLE)
          Losing a finger is nothing to the
          pain in the arm.

The bandage is in place. Sweat pours from Abdul's face but
his composure is good.

                    SHIR (SUBTITLE)
          You need to rest now.

Nak sees the finger and tosses it far away into the spinifex.

                    NAK (SUBTITLE)
          That's it, there's nothing further
          we can do for you. It's up to Allah
          now. If the paralysis in the arm
          gets any worse then I don't know
          what we can do.

                    ABDUL (SUBTITLE)
          My arm will have to come off, or
          I'll die.

> NAK (SUBTITLE)
> Then you'll die, Abdul, because I'm
> not strong enough to take off your
> arm.

Abdul looks at Shir with the question in his eyes.

> SHIR (SUBTITLE)
> I'm sorry, Abdul.
> (beat)
> We'll have to get you to a town or
> settlement.

> NAK (SUBTITLE)
> It'll be for another to decide,
> Abdul... not me or Shir. Only a
> doctor can help you further.

> ABDUL (SUBTITLE)
> What about your load of wool?

Nak looks at Shir.

> NAK (SUBTITLE)
> Maybe we can get it to Marree,
> maybe not. If your arm doesn't
> improve then we'll try and find
> help somewhere close.

> ABDUL (SUBTITLE)
> But your load. It'll be late
> getting to Marree.

> NAK (SUBTITLE)
> You're more important than a camel
> String loaded with supplies, Abdul.
> Besides, we're already behind
> schedule and would've missed the
> train already. The shipment will
> have to be sent with the next
> available train.

> ABDUL (SUBTITLE)
> Will Alfred be settled with that?

> NAK (SUBTITLE)
> Who cares?
> (beat)
> He knows as well as anyone else
> that you can't rule the weather
> conditions; besides, he knows that
> the wool will be delivered, even if
> a little late; he'll just have to
> suffer the inconvenience of getting
> paid a little less for his wool.

He'd not have done any better with
bullocks or horses; he knows that
as well and we do.

                ABDUL (SUBTITLE)
You're right, of course.
        (beat)
I think I'll try and get some sleep
now.

                NAK (SUBTITLE)
Yes... you do that.

Abdul gets up to fall upon his sleeping blanket. He looks one
last time at his friends at the camp fire.

                ABDUL (SUBTITLE)
Thank you... both.

                SHIR (SUBTITLE)
If you need anything, anything at
all, you just give the command and
I'll be there to help.

Abdul smiles and does his best to get comfortable upon his
blanket, hiding the true magnitude of his pain.

                                        DISSOLVE TO:

EXT. TENT - MIDNIGHT

Shir wakes to the sound of a bell, the stars out in all their
glory.

                SHIR (SUBTITLE)
What're you doing, Nak?

                NAK (SUBTITLE)
I took Slate's bell from around her
neck. Ringing it might help bring
some of the camels home.

                SHIR (SUBTITLE)
Home.
        (he scoffs)
A funny place to call home.

                NAK (SUBTITLE)
You know what I mean.

                SHIR (SUBTITLE)
So what're you going to do, ring
the bell all night?

                    NAK (SUBTITLE)
          I'll sleep, don't worry, and
          whenever I wake I'll ring the bell.

                    SHIR (SUBTITLE)
               (after a moment)
          I'll help. Let's take turns, Nak.
          Wake me when you're tired.

                    NAK (SUBTITLE)
          Thanks, Shir. That means a lot.
               (beat)
          I'm sorry about Slate and her calf.

                    SHIR (SUBTITLE)
          It's nothing we can control, so
          let's look after the things we can.

                    NAK (SUBTITLE)
          How's Abdul?

                    SHIR (SUBTITLE)
          He'll sleep for a long time yet. He
          didn't get much sleep during the
          storm.

                    NAK (SUBTITLE)
          His arm must be on the mend; I can
          hear him snoring. Let's pray that
          the infection clears up.

Nak goes back to ringing the bell, looking about the desert,
and Shir lays back down upon his blanket.

                                        DISSOLVE TO:

EXT. TENT - MORNING

Abdul wakes to find the sun rising and Shir cooking over the
camp fire. Abdul rubs his arm tenderly.

                    ABDUL (SUBTITLE)
          Good morning, Shir; and Before you
          ask, yes; I'm feeling better.

Abdul notices the saddle packs lined up where the camels were
to be concentrated and what appears to be all of the wool.

                    ABDUL (SUBTITLE) (CONT'D)
          I see you've managed to get the
          saddle packs ready.

Abdul walks towards the fire.

                    SHIR (SUBTITLE)
          There's still some equipment
          missing, but for the most part the
          wool was too heavy to shift far.
                    (beat)
          That storm was the worst I've ever
          experienced. Equipment has been
          blown up to two hundred feet away,
          and anything further afield won't
          be found.

                    ABDUL (SUBTITLE)
          Where's Nak?

                    SHIR (SUBTITLE)
          Looking for the camels.
                    (beat)
          Tell me the truth. Are you in much
          pain?

Abdul sits down besides Shir.

                    ABDUL (SUBTITLE)
          It's quite bad, but better than it
          was. How long's Nak been gone.

                    SHIR (SUBTITLE)
          Quite some time. I think Nak's
          leaning towards a day of rest.

                    ABDUL (SUBTITLE)
          Because of my arm? But the wool,
          it's got to get back to Marree.

                    SHIR (SUBTITLE)
          We're late as it is, any further
          delay won't alter the price at the
          depot. Our friend at the homestead
          was to be paid for delivery by
          deadline, not lateness in delivery.
          We'll just have to suffer the
          consequences this time around.

Shir looks up.

                    SHIR (SUBTITLE) (CONT'D)
          Ah, here's Nak now.

Both men see Nak returning with camels behind him, but Shir
can't see properly from where they sit.

                    ABDUL (SUBTITLE)
          Do you think we'll lose any
          contracts over this?

                    SHIR (SUBTITLE)
          No, but you can't ever tell.

Nak brings the camels into line near the saddle packs. Nak
waves on seeing Abdul, he waves back.

                    SHIR (SUBTITLE) (CONT'D)
          How many camels are missing?

Nak looks down the file, the camels one behind the other.

                    NAK (SUBTITLE)
          With what I've got here, that makes
          fourteen.

Nak looks to his friends.

                    NAK (SUBTITLE) (CONT'D)
          How's your arm, Abdul?

                    ABDUL (SUBTITLE)
          Better. I'll be able to work... I'm
          ready to work.

Nak comes closer to the fire, Shir hands him a plate of food.

                    NAK (SUBTITLE)
          I found three dead camels. The sand
          has covered everything. I saw
          several more camels about twenty
          minutes in that direction,
                    (he points)
          spooked by a dingo or two...
          there's no hope of getting them
          now. We'll have to double up on the
          stores each camel carries. They
          should be able to handle it so long
          as we don't push them too hard.

                    SHIR (SUBTITLE)
          They're good camels, every one.
          They'll carry the load, even if we
          have to make the days shorter.

                    ABDUL (SUBTITLE)
          Well... shall we make a start?

                    NAK (SUBTITLE)
          I want you to be sure, Abdul. Don't
          be a hero... I can't afford a hero.

                    ABDUL (SUBTITLE)
          I'm ready, Nak. I can't load or
          unload just yet, not efficiently,
                    (MORE)

                    (CONT'T)
          but I can hit with a stick if its
          needed; and walk, too.

                    NAK (SUBTITLE)
          We'll get going after breakfast.
          Just six hours on the road is all
          we'll do today. This will help the
          camels; and you, too, Abdul. We'll
          assess ourselves after that.

Abdul nods in appreciation and acceptance.

                    NAK (SUBTITLE) (CONT'D)
          I'm also taking the rifle back.
          With your arm the way it is... it
          will be of little use in your
          hands.

Abdul nods silently and we see Nak as he packs the rifle
where it's easy to access.

                                        DISSOLVE TO:

EXT. DESERT - DAY

An Aboriginal community is on the move, five men, four women,
and six children of between four and nine years of age, each
with something in their hand or upon their shoulder. We can
see vessels for the portage of water and tools for the
digging of roots; they have bags and bed rolls.

Flies in their hundreds are buzzing around the bed rolls and
blankets. The Aboriginals all have hard faces, are thin and
weary to the bone.

The women are quick to offer their hands for food, asking
silently for a handout.

The stench is terrible, Nak screws up his face. Abdul is next
in line and almost throws up. Abdul shakes his head and
coughs.

Shir is last to pass. He reaches into his pocket and throws a
portion of dried meat. Nak sees Shir's action, Shir sees Nak.

                    SHIR (SUBTITLE)
          They've lost everything in the
          storm Nak, just like us.

                    NAK (SUBTITLE)
          Yes, and we've nothing to spare. We
          have a long way to go, and they
          know how to hunt.

EXT. DESERT - LATE AFTERNOON

SERIES OF SHOTS

The sun grows hot.

Nak stumbles over a rock.

Shir's lips are cracking and he looks worst for wear.

Abdul stumbles slightly on a rock and winces with pain but continues on.

As we pull back from the scene we see that The caravan is a minute speck compared to the desert surrounds.

END SERIES OF SHOTS

EXT. GULLY - LATE AFTERNOON

The Afghans are being spied upon by five young men aged 18 to 20; SCOTTY, SNAKE, BULLOCK, HORSE and FLY. Their horses are tied up in the dry gully behind the tree line where the men lay in wait.

We move from one face to the other and see each in detail. Scotty has full cheeks and he's fat at the neck, he has meat on his bones and a double chin.

Snake is reasonably thin, a fighter through and through, a hard face for one so young.

Bullock is large, muscle bound and monstrous.

Horse has a baby face, full of kindness and maturity, seemingly untested by the harsh environment around.

Fly is short and thin, a heart filled with hatred for anyone remotely different than himself, a hatred which can be seen by the look in his eyes.

The caravan is still some distance off but can be seen for what it is. Scotty gets to his feet and moves to his horse, taking a can of bully beef from his saddle bag.

                    SCOTTY
          What do ya say to some Bully, Fly?
          Horse turns his head and looks back.

                    HORSE
          Shut ya mouth, you fool. Those damn
          freaks'll hear ya.

                    BULLOCK
          Calm down, Horse.

Bullock moves into the gully and towards his horse, along with Snake.

                    BULLOCK (CONT'D)
          They're still a ways off yet.

                    FLY
          I'm gonna clobber me one of those
          fellas, damn good.

                    SNAKE
          You and what army?

Snake pushes Fly where he lays, a stern look upon his face.

                    SCOTTY
          Shut up, Snake... why don't ya
          leave him alone.

                    FLY
          You don't have to defend me,
          Scotty. I might be the youngest but
          I can lick those men as good as
          anyone.

                    BULLOCK
          You won't need to, because I got
          me-self something hidden away.

Bullock draws a rifle from his bed roll.

                    HORSE
              (slightly panicked)
          Where the hell you get that?

                    BULLOCK
          It's me dad's rifle, ain't it.

                    HORSE
          You're not gonna use it, are ya?

                    BULLOCK
          Why the hell wouldn't I? What the
          hell do ya think I bought it for,
          if not to scare those buggers off
          our land once and for all?

                    FLY
          Scare them? We should shoot the
          bastards.

                    SCOTTY
          No, no, no. Ya don't wanna do that,
          Fly. We don't need no trouble with
          the law.

Snake takes a rifle from his bed roll, too.

                    SNAKE
          What law?

                    SCOTTY
               (nervously)
          What the.... What the hell you two
          doing?

                    SNAKE
          Look; if you don't want in; go
          home; but I'm staying. I've had
          enough of these bastards, coming
          here, taking me dad's work from
          underneath him.

                    HORSE
          They're just men. Scotty's right,
          we shouldn't be shooting 'em. The
          law'll get us all.

                    BULLOCK
          Look. The closest police is in
          Marree. We're not gonna get
          caught... not unless someone here
          tells on us... turns us in, maybe.

                    SCOTTY
          Don't look at me, Bullock. I'll do
          what you think is best, even if I
          don't like it.

                    FLY
          It's what they deserve.

                    SCOTTY
          I would've thought you had enough
          sense not to be so... stupid.

                    SNAKE
          Hey; he's with us... aren't ya,
          Fly?

                    FLY
          Sure am.
               (to Scotty)
          Ah, come on. Them fellas has been
          taking our fathers' work for ages.
          It's gotta stop.

                    BULLOCK
          He's right, Scotty. The lines gotta
          be drawn, once and for all.

                    FLY
          Come on, Scotty.

                    SCOTTY
          What do you think, Horse?

                    HORSE
          I don't know.

                    BULLOCK
          Ah, come on.

Horse moves into the gully.

                    HORSE
          I don't think we should. It ain't
          right.

                    SNAKE
          You're either with us or against
          us. If you're not with us then get
          on ya horse and go.

Horse looks around at everyone.

                    HORSE
          I'll go.

Horse mounts his horse.

                    BULLOCK
          You'll go south. I don't want them
          stinking camel herders to know
          we're here.

                    HORSE
          I got ya, Bullock. You don't need
          to tell me anything.
               (to Scotty)
          You should change your mind, before
          it's too late.

                    SNAKE
          Shut your mouth, Horse.

Horse kicks his horse and moves off, Scotty looks to the
ground and then at Bullock.

                    BULLOCK
          You're either in or out. What's it
          gonna be?

                    SCOTTY
               (after a moment)
          I'm in.

                    FLY
               (smiling)
          That's great, Scotty.

                    BULLOCK
          I'm glad, Scotty. I'm gonna tell ya
          something.

                    SCOTTY
          What's that, Bullock?

                    BULLOCK
          I saw these bastards down near
          Cooper just last week. I took up a
          position and watched them pass
          me... stinking camel bastards.

Bullock spits upon the ground.

                    BULLOCK (CONT'D)
          I've seen him before, the leader,
          the one with the scar across his
          face and mouth. I've heard about
          him, too. He was drinking our water
          from a small water hole.
               (beat)
          Do you remember last year when the
          dry spell hit us bad?

                    SCOTTY
          Sure.

                    BULLOCK
          That's when he was seen. But that
          was just for starters. That was
          when they were seen praying and
          they washed their damn feet in the
          water hole.

Bullock crawls back up to the tree line with his rifle in his
hand.

                    SCOTTY
          Those bastards.

                    BULLOCK
          That's right, Scotty. They cleaned
          their feet in our water, washed
          their bloody feet in it. That's
          bullshit.

                    SCOTTY
          Do ya think he deserves to die?

                    BULLOCK
          I do, for all he's done, for all
          the suffering we've gone through.

Snake looks over to Bullock.

                    SNAKE
          Come on, you ready or what? Pull
          back a bit so we can spread out
          proper.

The four boys now congregate in the low ground behind the
bush. Bullock points out their positions as he speaks.

                    BULLOCK
          Snake and me will go there, and
          there. Fly; you go there and Scotty
          just there.

Snake and Bullock take up a position so as to be closest to
the string when it first passes them by.

The string of 14 camels and three handlers is almost upon
them.

Fly is smiling, a sparkle in his eye.

EXT. TREE LINE - SAME

The lead camel is restless, looking off to the flank and the
tree line.

Nak follows the camel's gaze as Abdul looks up.

                    ABDUL (SUBTITLE)
          What is it?

                    NAK (SUBTITLE)
          I'm not sure.

Nak pulls the rope and hits his stick against the camel's
flank.

Suddenly a rifle shot explodes. The camels react accordingly,
four of them breaking their nose pegs.

                    ABDUL (SUBTITLE)
          Take cover!

Abdul hits the ground, forgetful of his finger, pain then
rivets throughout his arm. Nak, too, falls flat and looks to
the tree line in horror. A second shot suddenly rips through
the air, several more camels breaking free.

Nak scrambles to his feet and takes his rifle out.

                    NAK (SUBTITLE)
          Shir, are you okay?

Nak spins around, gets to his knee with rifle in hand and
looks to see Shir flat upon the ground.

                    BULLOCK
          NOW!

The four boys in hiding break from their cover and race
across the sixty feet of open ground.

Bullock looks to Snake who is first to reach the string and
slashes a rope between two camels.

                    ABDUL (SUBTITLE)
          Nak! Look out!

The kitchen camel pulls away and the line breaks. Camels are
running scared, lines breaking at their noses.

Snake looks down upon Shir and sees a great mass of blood
pouring from an exit wound in his back, saturating his shirt.
Abdul stands as Scotty and Fly dash about, slashing now at
the camels throats and jabbing at their bodies.

Snake collapses beside the dead Shir, shattered by his act of
murder.

                    SNAKE
               (sobbing slightly)
          What've I done?

Abdul kicks Fly in the leg and clenches his left fist.

                    ABDUL (SUBTITLE)
          You stinking heathen?

Abdul's face screws up in anger, Fly collapsing to the
ground, covering his face as he falls.

Scotty sees Abdul and reacts by stabbing him hard in the back
with his knife.

                    SCOTTY
          You stinking turd!

Abdul falls in a heap, screaming out in pain.

Fly manages to draw up alongside Scotty.

                    FLY
          Come on, Scotty!

They run back to the tree line.

Bullock reaches Nak and lashes out with his rifle butt, hitting Nak square in the jaw. Nak falls heavily as Bullock rips at a camel's nose peg. Nak recovers and reaches for his rifle.

Nak pulls the weapon into his shoulder, Bullock disappears between two camels which kick about and commence to run, free from their restraints. Nak sees Fly running and fires a shot.

An explosion is followed by Fly falling instantaneously, dead, his mouth open to the world.

SCOTTY
NO!

Scotty stops and goes to Fly's aid. He's tripped by Abdul who throws himself before him. Scotty's nose breaks and blood covers his face.

Snake recovers from his trauma and looks to Nak on hearing the rifle being fired. He sees Fly laying dead. A ghastly look falls over Snake's face.

EXT. DESERT - SAME

Horse is riding hard and fast, away from the tree line and gully. Suddenly he pulls to a halt on hearing a rifle shot in the distance.

He sits upon his horse motionless. He hears the second shot fill the air.

The third shot rings out and he pulls on the reigns and urges his mount on slowly towards where he has recently left his friends.

He stops and then starts once more towards them.

EXT. DESERT - LATER

Horse reaches a point just over halfway to the tree line when he hears a noise coming from behind some spinifex.

HORSE
Who's there?

Bullock lifts his head from behind the cover.

HORSE (CONT'D)
Bullock!

Snake then lifts his head, too.

Horse dismounts and races over to his friends who are crouched close by, stunned looks upon their faces.

Horse kneels down beside them.

                    HORSE (CONT'D)
          Where's Fly and Scotty?

Snake looks to the ground.

                    HORSE (CONT'D)
          Were they caught?

                    BULLOCK
          Scotty was captured.

                    HORSE
          And Fly?

                    SNAKE
               (flatly)
          He's dead.

                    BULLOCK
          We don't know that for sure.

Horse can see Bullock still has the rifle in his hand.

                    SNAKE
               (to Horse)
          I saw him.
               (to Bullock)
          Before I got away.

                    HORSE
               (to Snake)
          Where's your rifle?

                    BULLOCK
               (condescendingly)
          He left it behind.

Snake suddenly punches Bullock in the face before being set
upon by Horse.

                    HORSE
          That's enough; no more! Stop it! We
          should be more concerned about Fly
          and Scotty, not the bloody rifle.

                    SNAKE
          It's no good. Fly's dead; I know
          it. When I heard the rifle shot, I
          looked up and saw Fly fall. Scotty
          fell down after that, but I think
          he's okay.

                    HORSE
          So what happened to your rifle?

                    SNAKE
          I guess I dropped it.

                    BULLOCK
          Dropped it!

Snake takes up a stance, ready for a fight with Bullock, but
Horse gets between them.

                    HORSE
          Enough! We gotta think now. We
          can't just leave Scotty there with
          those bastards.

                    SNAKE
          I don't think I can do any more. I
          feel sick inside.

                    HORSE
          You should have thought about that
          earlier, but now... it's too
          late... we have to help Scotty.

                    BULLOCK
          I still got my rifle.

                    HORSE
               (thinking)
          I don't know. They have two, we've
          only got one.

                    BULLOCK
               (bravely)
          We'll shoot first.

                    SNAKE
          This isn't funny, Bullock!

                    BULLOCK
          No one said it was. We have ta go
          in armed, we have no choice now.

                    HORSE
          You're right. I don't think we have
          a choice.

                    SNAKE
               (beat)
          I killed one of them.

                    BULLOCK
          Don't feel guilty, Snake. They got
          at least one of us, too. I think we
          should finish this and get back to
          Mulka.

                    HORSE
          He's right. We have to save Scotty.

Horse looks around.

                    HORSE (CONT'D)
          Where's your horses? They lost?

                    SNAKE
          We don't have 'em, the Afghans do.

                    HORSE
          Then we'll have to get them back as
          well.

EXT. GULLY - LATER

Shir's body is wrapped in a blanket, laying beneath a tree,
flies starting to congregate around his corpse.

                    NAK (SUBTITLE)
          The flies I hate the most. Forever
          in our faces; and now poor Shir's
          dead and they want some of him.

                    ABDUL (SUBTITLE)
          What about that one?

Nak looks over at the corpse of Fly; his body is unwrapped.

                    NAK (SUBTITLE)
          Let the maggots have their feast
          upon his rotting carcass.
               (beat)
          How's your back?

                    ABDUL
                    (SUBTITLE)
          It's not too bad. The knife hardly
          touched me. Besides, it takes my
          mind off the scorpion bite.

                    NAK (SUBTITLE)
          Is it very painful?

                    ADBUL (SUBTITLE)
          Nowhere near as bad as it was. My
          arm is getting better... slowly.

Nak looks now to the other boy sitting with his back against a tree, his hands bound.

                    NAK
          What you name?

Scotty has a broken nose, blood smears over his face, and two black eyes.

Nak stands up and looks to race over towards Scotty.

                    SCOTTY
          SCOTTY! My name's Scotty!

Nak sits back down.

                    NAK
          You friend coward, run quick, much
          far away now. Horses now mine, you
          nothing. I get pretty good money
          from horse.

                    ABDUL (SUBTITLE)
          I don't think he cares. I saw him
          slash a camel's throat. I'm sure
          he's the same one that stabbed me
          in the back.
               (beat)
          What're we to do now?

                    NAK (SUBTITLE)
          We'll have to tell the police, and
          hand the boy over. I don't see any
          other alternative. I don't exactly
          trust the police but what choice do
          we have?
               (beat)
          We can't let the boy go because
          he'll tell lies and we could end up
          being convicted of murder, but with
          the boy in custody, along with the
          horses, I think we can fairly well
          sell our story of self defense.

Abdul looks over to the body of Fly.

                    ABDUL (SUBTITLE)
          Don't you think we should cover the
          boy's body before the maggots eat
          too much? The police won't take
          kindly to us leaving him to be
          eaten like this. His parents will
          take unkindly...

                    NAK (SUBTITLE)
          (interrupting)
I don't care, Abdul!
          (beat)
The people here can think what they
like. I'm sick to death of them
all. Even those we serve have
condemned our beliefs by smuggling
bacon upon the loads we carry. None
of them can be trusted.

                    ABDUL (SUBTITLE)
When will we leave?

                    NAK (SUBTITLE)
Tomorrow morning. We'll take the
few camels we have along with the
horses. The horses can be used to
carry the dead; the prisoner we'll
make walk for a while but let him
ride later, so the police don't
think too badly of us, but I want
him tired. I want to be away from
here as soon as possible.

                    ABDUL (SUBTITLE)
What about the other camels; the
lost?

                    NAK (SUBTITLE)
They'll have to stay lost. We have
to move quickly. Maybe we can come
back for them later.

                    ABDUL (SUBTITLE)
In that case, wouldn't it be best
to collect the wool together and
leave it all here? We'll hardly be
able to get enough back to Marree
now.

                    NAK (SUBTITLE)
You're right.
          (beat)
I'll consider it all tonight.

                    ABDUL (SUBTITLE)
You realize that the other boys
might come back, and from my
recollection they still have a
rifle.

                    NAK (SUBTITLE)
We have two.
          (MORE)

                    (CONT'D)
          (beat)
We've currently just three camels
left and four horses. We've no food
and little water. My Koran is gone
and the prayer mats, too.
          (beat)
That Scotty bastard can stay where
he is for the night and suffer the
cold.
          (beat)
Get a fire going, Abdul.

              ABDUL (SUBTITLE)
And the other's; the boys?

              NAK (SUBTITLE)
We'll maintain watch, just like
when in the army. We can set up a
small watching post over that way.

Nak points.

              NAK (SUBTITLE) (CONT'D)
The others headed to the south and
I want good visual to be maintained
with the rising of the sun. If they
approach the fire then they have to
be shot; we can't afford to be
caught unaware.

              ABDUL (SUBTITLE)
They have the advantage.

              NAK (SUBTITLE)
We have a prisoner and two rifles.

              ABDUL (SUBTITLE)
You know... I'm not afraid to die,
just concerned for my family back
home. They'll never know what
happened to me. I just think its
more kind for them to know what I
did here, and that I didn't just
abandon them.

              NAK (SUBTITLE)
Your wife loves you, Abdul. She'll
not think unkindly.

              ABDUL (SUBTITLE)
And what about you, Nak? Are you
afraid to die?

                    NAK (SUBTITLE)
          There's life after death, dear
          friend. I'll be thirty-two years
          old once more; for eternity; and
          have seventy-two virgins to appease
          my every need. What more could a
          man ask for?

Abdul gives a little laugh.

                    ABDUL (SUBTITLE)
          It's good for you. You're forty-two
          at present and get a good deal if
          you die; I'm only twenty-three so
          gain nine years.

                    NAK (SUBTITLE)
          But you also gain many virgins.
               (beat)
          Being married... That will have an
          affect on your ability to enjoy
          seventy-two virgins.

                    ABDUL (SUBTITLE)
               (smiling)
          You're right. It's too many virgins
          for me. Maybe I'll give you some of
          mine.

                    NAK (SUBTITLE)
          My dear friend, Abdul, even
          seventy-two virgins is to good for
          me, any more and I'll die a second
          death.

A serious look now falls over Abdul.

                    ABDUL (SUBTITLE)
          Nak... there's something I have to
          tell you.

                    NAK (SUBTITLE)
          What?

                    ABDUL (SUBTITLE)
          It's about the battle of Char
          Asiab.

                    NAK (SUBTITLE)
          So you fought with the British and
          I against them. It doesn't matter,
          Abdul. It's okay; it's forgotten.

                    ABDUL (SUBTITLE)
          No, something else.

                    NAK (SUBTITLE)
          What? What else is there?

                    ABDUL (SUBTITLE)
          That scar on your face; your lips.

Nak gently passes his finger tips over the horrendous scar
tissue.

                    ABDUL (SUBTITLE) (CONT'D)
          It was me, Nak. I was the one that
          fired the shot that wounded you.

Nak looks at Abdul closely and waves the thought away.

                    NAK (SUBTITLE)
          No. You're mistaken.

                    ABDUL (SUBTITLE)
          I was in Char Asiab. I was in
          conflict with you, Nak. I saw you
          get out from your defensive
          position... I saw the injury upon
          your face...
                    (beat)
          I saw your face, Nak... I know it
          was you.

                    NAK (SUBTITLE)
          It could have been any man that
          fired that shot. There was a lot of
          bullets flying through the air...
          It could have been anyone.

Abdul smiles lightly and holds out his hand. Nak hesitates
and then accepts it.

                    ABDUL (SUBTITLE)
          I'm sorry, Nak... truly sorry for
          the pain I've caused you this many
          years.

They hold hands for a few seconds and then release their
hold.

                    NAK (SUBTITLE)
          It wasn't you, Abdul. And even it
          it was... I forgive you. You're my
          friend, Nak; as true a friend could
          ever be; now and forever.

EXT. DESERT - SAME

Snake, Bullock, and Horse are on foot, Horse leads his mount
along by the reins in his hand. Snake puts his hand up and

they all come to a halt.

                    BULLOCK
          What is it? What do you see?

                    SNAKE
          A camel.

Bullock lifts his rifle into his shoulder. Horse slams his
hand down upon the barrel, unsettling his friend.

                    HORSE
          Don't be foolish; idiot.

                    BULLOCK
          Damn! You're the idiot. What'd you
          do that for? I've got a good mind
          to smash you in the face.

                    HORSE
          Why don't ya try, shit-for-brains?

                    SNAKE
          Because it's what the bastard
          cameleers want.

                    HORSE
          No shooting, Bullock; not yet.

                    SNAKE
          Hey, I got a better idea.

Snake takes an axe handle from Horse's saddle pack and heads
off slowly towards the camel.

                    HORSE
          What are you doing now?

                    SNAKE
          Do you want these camels to fester
          the land you call home?

Snake approaches the camel, the others watch on, the sun
commences to fall beyond the horizon.

The camel is busy eating, ignoring Snake. Snake turns to look
at the others with a smile on his face and then turns again
to the camel.

Snake is close enough now and gets a good grip on the axe
handle. He swings and commences to bash the camels head in.
The camel falls, unsettling noises erupting from within.
Snake keeps up the bashing until satisfied. He looks down
upon the bloody animal and spits upon it.

                    BULLOCK
          Come on, Snake, that's enough. It's
          dead now.

                    SNAKE
          I'm sick of these bloody animals.
          Good for nothing is what they are.

Horse draws alongside.

                    HORSE
          We're all sick of them, Snake. We
          all suffer.

                    SNAKE
          And now its time they suffered.
          We'll wait till it gets dark;
          they'll have to light a fire sooner
          or later: won't they?

                    HORSE
          I sure hope so, otherwise poor old
          Scotty's going to have a terrible
          night.

                    SNAKE
          Don't you mean, Scotty and Fly?

                    HORSE
          Yeah... yeah; that's exactly what I
          mean.

                    SNAKE
          Well, lets see if we can't help
          them out a little. Come on, let's
          get out of here; this camel stinks.

                                        DISSOLVE TO:

EXT. GULLY - NIGHT

The sky is filled with stars.

Abdul is sitting next to a large bush and facing towards
where the campfire burns low and bright, the brightness
evaporating into the night and extinguishing itself, the edge
between light and dark very distinct.

Abdul pulls the blanket tight around him, the rifle in his
lap. He has the second rifle by his right side.

Nak rolls over in his blanket and Scotty is stretched out
under the tree, trying to get his feet warmed by the fire.

Scotty has a gag in his mouth.

A noise is heard in the distance, a stick snapping. Abdul cocks his head.

A horse can be heard to whinny once and then silence once more surrounds him.

Suddenly he sees a silhouette. Someone is approaching very slowly and carefully.

We see Scotty fast asleep. another two silhouettes then appear out of nowhere. The first of the figures now becomes partially illuminated by the fire. One of them is carrying a rifle. We see Nak is still asleep.

Abdul lifts his rifle and takes aim down the sights. He shoots at the boy he thinks has the rifle, the explosion waking Nak and Scotty, but Abdul misses and hits Snake instead. Snake falls down, shot in the stomach.

Horse and Bullock take cover, heavy gasping erupts from Snake. Nak springs to his feet as Bullock brings his rifle into his shoulder and Bullock shoots Abdul in the right shoulder.

                    ABDUL
          Ahhh!

Nak takes cover and Abdul drops his rifle, he then quickly takes up the second, wincing with pain. Scotty curls into a ball, Horse moves up level with Bullock, and Bullock tries to ready his rifle for another shot.

                    ABDUL (SUBTITLE) (CONT'D)
          Take cover, Nak!

Abdul pulls the trigger and hits Bullock square in the head, killing him instantly. The body drops to the ground with a heavy thud.

                    HORSE
          Bullock!

Horse jumps over to where Bullock now lays and picks up his rifle, searching the prostrate body frantically for some ammunition.

Nak rolls out of the way and gets to his feet before stalling and then charging Horse.

Snake is on the ground and kicks out his leg, Nak falls over it to within several feet of Horse. A blade of spinifex grass is forced into Nak's left eye.

                    NAK
          Arrghh!

The flickering light of the fire paints a ghastly look upon
Snake's face. Snake gasps for air and then dies.

Horse loads his weapon. He lifts the rifle into his shoulder
and shoots Nak dead. The explosion fills the air and then
there is silence.

The flickering light of the fire makes it hard to see.

                    ABDUL (SUBTITLE)
          NAK! NAK! Where are you?

Abdul watches his front. His left hand momentarily goes to
the aid of the pain in his shoulder. He now picks up some
ammunition and reloads his weapon before taking up the second
and repeats the action.

We hear the rifles being loaded along with the crackling of
the fire.

Horse throws his spent rifle down and races over to Scotty
who is now kicking on the ground for attention, muffled
sounds coming from behind the gag in his mouth.

                    HORSE
          It's okay, Scotty; it's me; keep
          still.

Horse is now kneeling beside Scotty and pulls a knife from
its sheaf before cutting Scotty's bonds and then removing his
gag.

                    SCOTTY
          Be careful, Horse.

We see Abdul aiming at Horse and then he moves his sights to
fall upon Scotty. Without further thought or hesitation, he
squeezes the trigger of the weapon in his hand and kills
Scotty outright, a perfect shot to the head.

                    HORSE
          NO!!

Horse collapses, sobbing, punching the ground once with a
clenched fist.

Abdul takes up the other rifle. He watches his front and sees
Horse bent over Scotty's body.

                    ABDUL
          YOU! You listen to me! You go. You
          go long way, no come back. You get
          horse, you take, you go home. Me
          forget quick. Me not care. You
                    (MORE)

                    (CONT'D)
          live, me live; both live. You know
          what meaning is?

                    HORSE
               (snarling)
          Yes. I know exactly what you mean.

Horse looks again at Scotty amidst the flickering light. His
dead friend has his eyes closed.

                    HORSE (CONT'D)
          You've killed four of my friends.
          That'll be hard to live with.

                    ABDUL
          You start killing us and camels, we
          are good people, give harm to no
          one. But now... alive is good, dead
          is bad. You go and me go. Both go
          home.

There is a moment of silence.

                    HORSE
          Yes.

Horse stands and sheaves his knife.

                    HORSE (CONT'D) (CONT'D)
          We both go.

                    ABDUL
          You do thing, one more. You make
          horse speak, me know you gone long
          way.

                    HORSE
          Yes; yes, okay. But I'll be back
          tomorrow, to get my friends. If
          you're still here then I'll kill
          you.

                    ABDUL
          Okay. I go quick too.

Abdul watches as Horse turns and moves away from the camp
fire and silence again returns to the scene.

                                        DISSOLVE TO:

EXT. DESERT - DAY

Abdul is on foot and staggers a little as he makes his way
south. His wound is hastily dressed.

Nak and Shir are strapped to two camels, a third carries
little more than the makeshift tent and some water. The heat
continues to grow, glimmering waves of heat dancing across
the desert.

Abdul looks down upon the ground as he walks, unable to see
the shadow cast by his body, the sun high above.

He trips over a rock and bangs his head upon the ground. He
moves his good hand to his forehead. Blood now starts to seep
from his shoulder wound more than before. His hold on the
camels is lost and they commence to wonder off with the
bodies of Nak and Shir strapped to them. Abdul falls
unconscious as the camels continue into the depths of the
desert.

                                        DISSOLVE TO:

EXT. DESERT - AFTERNOON

The jolting of the wagon wakes Abdul up, and as he stirs a
familiar voice echoes in his ear. Jacob is seated in the
front of a wagon and Abdul is laying in the back. Jacob is
speaking in German.

                    JACOB (SUBTITLE)
            Ah, praise the good lord that you
            have risen. You've been in and out
            of your daze all day now. How do
            you feel?

Abdul rubs his eyes and is suddenly reminded of his pain in
his shoulder, which shows upon his face.

                    JACOB (SUBTITLE) (CONT'D)
            Ah; I fixed that as best I could. I
            stopped the bleeding, but it took
            some time.

Abdul tries to speak the best English he can.

                    ABDUL
            Where we go?

                    JACOB
            Ah... I find you... in track, ah. I
            go to Marree, is close.

                    JACOB (SUBTITLE) (CONT'D)
            It's the least I can do for a
            religious man, even if it goes
            against the grain.

                    ABDUL
Where friend?

                    JACOB (SUBTITLE)
Friend? Ah; other men?

                    JACOB (CONT'D)
I do not know... ah... they Are
gone.

                    JACOB (SUBTITLE) (CONT'D)
I thought it was strange that they
should leave you alone like that.
Did one of them shoot you?

                    JACOB (CONT'D)
Friend is bang bang you; he leave?

                    ABDUL
No. No friends? They dead.

                    JACOB
          (confused)
Are they dead?
          (beat)
I not know?

                    ABDUL
No, no. Not meaning. I tell is
true. Friend is dead; you find; you
see them and camels?

Jacob hands Abdul a water canteen.

                    JACOB (SUBTITLE)
Here, have a drink. No, I didn't
see anyone. No camels, no friends.
Just you; and lucky I came across
you when I did otherwise you'd be
dead.
          (beat)
We shouldn't be long into Marree.

                    JACOB (CONT'D)
No friends, I see no camels. We go
to Marree, go to police and tell.

                    ABDUL
No! No, is okay.

                    JACOB (SUBTITLE)
No! Well... it's up to you, of
course. But it seems to me that
justice should be delivered those
                    (MORE)

                    (CONT'D)
          that left you in the desert to
          die.

Jacob shrugs his shoulders

                    JACOB (CONT'D)
          No... Okay; go Marree, no police,
          is okay?

                    ABDUL
          Yes; This good. Forgive, and
          forget. But is never forget good
          man; good Jacob. You good friend.
          You good man this place. Me never
          forget. Me go home, now, go
          Afghanistan, no more Australia. No
          more for me; is finished.

Jacob turns his attention to driving the bullock team.
We pull back from the scene as the desert takes up the
picture, the wagon now nothing more than a speck upon an
ocean of desert and dry spinifex.

                                        FADE OUT.

              THE END